Jonas was impeccably dressed.

Kat's eyes traveled over a broad chest and wide shoulders, up a tanned neck, to a strong jaw covered with two-day-old stubble. A mouth that was slow to smile but still sexy. Rich, successful and hot.

He had a rep for being a bit of a bastard, in business and in bed. That fact only dropped his sexy factor by a quarter of a percent.

"Mr. Halstead, welcome back to El Acantilado," Kat murmured, ignoring her jumping heart.

"Call me Jonas."

It wasn't the first time he'd made the offer, but Kat had no intention of accepting. It wasn't professional, and formality kept a healthy distance between her and guys in fancy suits. Like her ex-husband, and sadly, just like her father, those kinds of men were not to be trusted.

But it really annoyed Kat that a thousand sparks danced on her skin as Jonas's smile turned his face from remote-but-still-hot to oh-my-God-I want-to-rip-his-clothes-off.

No. Sexy billionaires were *not* her type. She'd married, and divorced, a ruthless and merciless rich guy.

But it sure felt like she had the screaming hots for a man she shouldn't.

And it was all Jonas Halstead's fault.

* * *

Convenient Cinderella Bride is part of the Secrets of the A-List series: When you have it all, you'll do anything to keep it.

Dear Reader,

Welcome to sunny Santa Barbara and the wealthy world of the West Coast. *Convenient Cinderella Bride* is a spinoff of the Secrets of the A-List series, where I introduced readers to the fabulously wealthy and furiously complicated world of Harrison Marshall and his charismatic family. In Secrets of the A-List, Harrison's secrets, and there are many, are slowly revealed, and each new secret is another scandal the much-watched family has to navigate.

In *Convenient Cinderella Bride*, Jonas Halstead—Harrison's friend and business rival—has his own problems to deal with, thanks to his demanding grandfather. Jack has decided that, in order to inherit the controlling shares of Halstead International, Jonas must marry. And within three months. Jonas cannot believe that his grandfather is acting like a medieval warlord, but Jack isn't budging, so marry he must.

Kat Morrison, a hostess at Harrison's famous restaurant, El Alcantilado, has her own problems and they revolve around a lack of money. An ugly divorce and finding out that her father, after his death, left everything—including her own mother's possessions—to her stepmom caused Kat's trust levels to plummet and her independence levels to rise. There are two things she knows for sure: the only person she can rely on is herself, and she will never marry again.

I loved writing Jonas and Kat's happily-ever-after in Santa Barbara and intertwining their lives with that of the fascinating Marshalls. Connect with me at www.josswoodbooks.com, on Twitter, @josswoodbooks, and Facebook at Joss Wood Author.

Happy reading,

Joss

JOSS WOOD

CONVENIENT CINDERELLA BRIDE

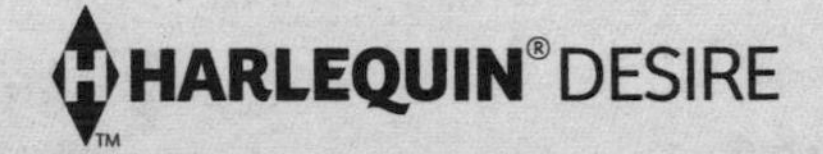

Special thanks and acknowledgment are given to Joss Wood for her contribution to the Secrets of the A-List miniseries.

Recycling programs for this product may not exist in your area.

ISBN-13: 978-0-373-83869-1

Convenient Cinderella Bride

This edition published by arrangement with Harlequin Books S.A.

For questions and comments about the quality of this book, please contact us at CustomerService@Harlequin.com.

Printed in U.S.A.

Joss Wood loves books and traveling—especially to the wild places of southern Africa. She has the domestic skills of a potted plant and drinks far too much coffee.

Joss has written for Harlequin KISS, Harlequin Presents and, most recently, the Harlequin Desire line. After a career in business, she now writes full-time. Joss is a member of the Romance Writers of America and Romance Writers of South Africa.

Books by Joss Wood

Harlequin Desire

Secrets of the A-List

Convenient Cinderella Bride

From Mavericks to Married

Trapped with the Maverick Millionaire
Pregnant by the Maverick Millionaire
Married to the Maverick Millionaire

The Ballantyne Billionaires

His Ex's Well-Kept Secret
The Ballantyne Billionaires
The CEO's Nanny Affair

Visit her Author Profile page at Harlequin.com, or josswoodbooks.com, for more titles.

One

Another month, another breakfast. How many of these business breakfasts had they shared? Jonas Halstead had been the CEO of Halstead & Sons for five years… He did the calculation. Sixty Wednesday breakfasts.

Sixty three-hour meetings with the man commonly known as "The White Shark of the West Coast." Jack was reputed to be the most ruthless, occasionally morally ambiguous, businessman on this side of the country. He was also Jonas's grandfather, and Jonas would rather be water-boarded than sit through this monthly meeting.

When he'd first started as CEO he'd banned his staff from dealing directly with the chairman of the board because few people could deal with Jack's harsh manner, his interrogations and his dire warnings about possible disaster situations. Few, even those who were corporate animals, could handle Jack's aggression and his pursuit of perfection. Jonas had long ago realized that if he wanted to keep his key staff then he had to shield them from Jack.

But that meant it was his ass in the hot seat.

Jonas was a big boy, being paid the big bucks. He could deal with Jack. But, hell, he could not wait for the day when he could run Halstead & Sons without Jack's constant input and criticism. Thanks to Jack's ruthlessness and Jonas's father's reputation for cutting corners, the Halstead name was not one to be trusted, and while that didn't bother Jack in the least—*Let the bastards fear us, it's good for business!*—Jonas hated having his word doubted, his integrity questioned. He was a hard, tough businessman. He drove a hard bargain. But when he gave his word, he kept it. Always.

His family had a reputation for doing legal but morally dodgy deals, for losing their integrity in pursuit of the mighty dollar. Promises were broken; lies were told. Seeing the instinctual mistrust on the faces of his investors, suppliers and competitors burned a hole in his stomach and still, quietly and secretly, embarrassed the hell out of him. He was determined to rehabilitate the company's reputation and was just as committed to establishing his own reputation as a man whose word could be trusted.

He thought, maybe, that he was making progress, but it was taking a hell of a long time.

Having Jack still serving as chairman of the board didn't help. But, dammit, it was Jack's company, and until he decided to release the reins, Jonas could only manage the old man. And keep his treasured staff away from him.

Jonas walked up the steps to Jack's palatial, beach-side home on the prestigious Palisade Beach Road in Santa Monica. The house had been in the Halstead family for many generations, long before Hollywood's elite had discovered the area. Jonas had grown up here. Well, in this house and the one next door, spending his time between his father's and grandfather's mansions, a motherless boy looking for attention from his disinterested father and demanding grandfather.

Jonas entered the spacious hallway and greeted Henry, his grandfather's man-about-the-house. Wanting to get this meeting over with, Jonas made his way through the Spanish Colonial Revival mansion to the outside entertainment area with its one-hundred-eighty-degree view of the beach and the ocean. The wind was up and the waves were high, perfect conditions for a bit of surfing or kitesurfing. Jonas jogged down the steps from the entertainment area to the tiled patio at the edge of the property, which held comfortable chairs and expensive outdoor furniture. Despite the distance from the kitchen, this tree-shaded spot was Jack's favorite place to dine.

His grandfather sat at the head of the table, his hand wrapped around a coffee cup, his glasses perched on the end of his nose, reading the business section of the paper, a daily habit of his. Jack liked his habits, in business and in his personal life. He wasn't fond of people—sons, grandsons, colleagues and staff—coloring outside the lines. Jonas's fluid, going-with-his-gut way of managing Halstead & Sons was a constant source of irritation to his grandfather. Jack could be as disapproving as he liked, but he couldn't argue with the numbers; since taking over as CEO of Halstead five years ago, cash flow and profits had steadily increased.

Jonas noticed Preston McIntyre. Why was Jack's lawyer eating with them? Jonas shook Preston's hand and slid a glance in Jack's direction. He immediately recognized the stubborn I'll-get-to-it-when-I'm-ready expression. There was no point in pushing; the old man was as stubborn as a mule. Which grated, since Jonas was a get-it-done-now type of guy.

Jonas pulled out a chair from the table. "Morning, Jack."

He'd been Grandpa Jack when Jonas had been younger, but it had been a while since he'd called his grandfather anything but his given name. Jack wasn't the sentimental type. "Jonas. Have some breakfast."

Jonas reached for the fruit salad.

"How is Cliff House coming along?" Jack demanded, his eyes flashing.

The Cliff House was their newest project, a rambling, neglected property that had once been the most luxurious hotel in Santa Barbara. That had been in the 1920s and it was now just a mess and a money pit. But it had awesome views and potential, and, best of all, Jonas had bought the property out from under Harrison Marshall's nose. Harrison might be a world-renowned chef, restaurateur and family friend, but going onto his turf and snagging a property he'd desperately wanted had been fun. And it had been a clean snatch; a simple offer of more money that the owner had quickly accepted.

"On time and on budget," Jonas replied, knowing that was all Jack wanted to hear. And it was the truth. He ran a tight ship.

"That's the least I expect," Jack snapped, eyes flashing. "Elaborate."

Jonas gave Jack his verbal report, his eyes flicking to the smaller but still impressive house next door. The windows were locked and the drapes were closed. That meant his father was in Europe looking for art that could be added to his already extensive collection.

Such wealth, Jonas thought, was attached to his surname. The houses, the cars…the option not to work another day in his life—that's the choice his father had made.

Jonas shuddered. Work was what gave his life meaning, how he filled his days. It provided the context of his life, the framework that kept him sane. For him, having nothing to do would be a nightmare.

He was too driven, too intense, too ambitious. In that way, he was like his grandfather. A focused workaholic determined to grow the family company under his stewardship. Besides, what else would he do with his time? He didn't have—didn't want—a wife and kids, and he didn't play golf.

Jonas wondered, as he often did, if he would be as driven if he'd had a gentler upbringing, if he hadn't had his father and grandfather riding him to do better, to be better. They'd both assumed he would be the future of the company, the fifth Halstead to run their multigenerational empire. A lot of emphasis had been placed on his performance; success was praised, failure was disparaged and a perceived lack of effort ignited tempers. Jack had encouraged independence of thought and deed, and winning at all costs. Lane, his father, didn't believe in expressing any emotion. As a child, Jonas had learned to suppress his feelings. They were tools his father used to mock or denigrate him. It was easier, he'd discovered, to avoid emotional neediness in both himself and others.

Jack asked him another series of questions and Jonas concentrated on the here and now. There was no point in looking back, it didn't achieve anything. And since Jack was, technically, Jonas's boss, he needed to concentrate. His position was reasonably secure. He'd pulled the company into the twenty-first century and both stocks and profit margins were up. He had the Halstead name, but he didn't own the company. Yet.

Jack leaned back in his chair, asked Jonas to pour coffee and Jonas complied. Preston had said nothing for the past half hour and Jonas wondered, again, why he was there. Preston gave him an uneasy look, and Jonas knew he was about to find out. And he wasn't going to like it.

What was his wily grandfather plotting?

Jonas watched his grandfather, who was looking down the beach.

Jack's deep green eyes, the same color as Jonas's, eventually settled on his grandson's face. "I am re-writing my will."

Jonas felt his stomach knot. Dammit, again? They went through this every five years or so. As far as Jonas knew, he would inherit Jack's shares in the company and his father would inherit a massive life insurance policy and most of Jack's personal properties, excluding this house.

"This property and my shares in the company will all be yours."

Good. He'd be pissed if he'd worked sixteen hours a day for more than a decade for nothing. "Thank you," he said, knowing that was the only response Jack wanted or would tolerate.

"But..."

Oh, crap.

"...only if you marry within the next ninety days."

What the hell?

It took every iota of Jonas's self-control not to react. He wanted to leap to his feet, slam his hands on the table and demand that Jack explain his crazy statement. He wanted to ask his grandfather if he'd lost his marbles. But the only gesture of annoyance he allowed himself was the tightening of his grip around his coffee cup.

"That's a hell of a demand, Jack," Jonas said, danger creeping into his tone. "Does it come with an explanation?"

"You're pissed," Jack said, and Jonas caught the note of amusement in his voice.

"Wouldn't you be?" Jonas countered, straining to keep his tone even.

"Sure," Jack agreed. "You can be as pissed as you like, but I'm not changing my mind. You're going to marry or you lose it all."

Jonas rubbed his forehead, not quite believing how Jack had flipped Jonas's life on its head in the space of five minutes. Jonas turned to Preston. "Is this legal?"

Preston sent him a sympathetic look. "They are his assets. He's allowed to disperse them any way he likes. It's blackmail but its legal blackmail."

Preston narrowed his eyes at his client and Jonas's respect for the lawyer increased.

"I've made up my mind," Jack said, ignoring his lawyer's comment. "Marry in ninety days and I will sign over everything to you, giving you complete control of the company and ownership of this house. That way we'll avoid paying the state a ridiculous amount of money in estate tax. All you have to do is marry."

"And if I don't?"

"Your father will inherit my shares. He wants them and feels they're his right as the next in line." Jack's voice was as hard as nails. "He has expressed his wish to return to the company."

Jonas struggled to look through the red mist in front of his eyes. He hastily bit back the words *over my dead body.*

"He is a Halstead, Jonas. He says he's bored, that it's time for him to come back and take his place as the next Halstead to run our company."

But Lane stole from the company to support his gambling habit! The words were on the tip of Jonas's tongue but he couldn't voice them. Who was he protecting by keeping Lane's secret? Jack? His father? Himself?

"He walked away, Jack." It was all he could say in protest.

"He's still a talented businessman. And my son."

"And all the work I've done in the years since he left has meant nothing? You'd do this without my consent?" Jonas saw the answer on Jack's face and shook his head. "You're a piece of work."

Jack just shrugged. "My first priority will always be what I think is best for Halstead."

Of course it was, God forbid that he put his grandson's wishes before his company. "You have done a reasonable job with the company," Jack continued, "but what, or who, comes after you? In your twenties, you dated extensively and I wasn't worried. I believed you needed time to sow your wild oats. But you're about to turn thirty-five, you've never brought a girl home to meet me and I'm concerned you will never settle down."

"You've been single for more than fifty years,

so I think it's a bit hypocritical for you to judge my lifestyle," Jonas pointed out.

"I was married. I produced a Halstead heir and Lane did the same. You have not. You should be married. You should have had a child or two by now."

"These days, people are marrying and having children later in life, Jack!"

Jack glared at him. "I want to see you married. I want to see your child. I want to be assured that the Halstead fortune will not pass out of our bloodline."

"I'm surprised you didn't demand that I produce a child in three months, as well," Jonas snapped.

"I'm not *that* demanding. That being said, if you marry, then there's a good chance children will come from the union," Jack said, stubbornness in every word he spoke. "Eventually. And I know you well enough to know that you'd hate, as much as I do, the idea of Halstead money, generations of effort and hard work, benefiting someone not of our bloodline."

Bloodline? Jack sounded like a medieval lord talking about his estates. "This isn't sixteenth century England, Jack. And I do not appreciate you meddling in my private life!"

"Pffft! Arranged marriages have worked for hundreds of years before love clouded the issue. It's simple, Jonas. Marry and I will give you Halstead. Do not and deal with your father."

Jonas muttered a low curse. Jack knew exactly what buttons to push; he knew Jonas would do anything to keep his father out of the company and that he wanted complete control of Halstead & Sons.

But there was a price to that freedom and the price was marriage. The one thing he'd planned to avoid for as long as possible.

But Jack had left him without a choice. It was Jack's way or the highway.

Jonas pushed his chair back, tossed his linen napkin onto the table and leaned across to shake Preston's hand. He ignored his grandfather, too angry with him to speak. He started to walk away but Jack's voice followed him.

"Well, what are you going to do?" he demanded.

Jonas relished the note of uncertainty in his voice.

He slowly turned and eyed his elderly relative, his smile cold. "I'll guess you'll find out in three months. You can wait until then."

Katrina Morrison slid her hand beneath her hair and, discreetly, pushed her finger under the seam of her dress, moving the still attached price tag in the hope that it would stop scratching her skin. How she wished she was in the position to yank the tag off and be done with it. But Tess, her best friend, who happened to be the manager of The Hanger—a downtown Santa Barbara boutique selling designer dresses—would slap her silly if she did that. Tess still had to sell the dresses Kat had "borrowed."

God knew what Tess would do if she ripped the dress or spilled wine or food on it. Katrina would probably be tarred and feathered at dawn.

Or, worse, she'd have to pay for the dress. And she didn't have a thousand-plus dollars to spare. Even if she did have that sort of cash lying around, Kat doubted she'd spend it on a mid-thigh, sleeveless, pleated dress that was so understated it screamed "expensive." But appearances, especially when you were the host at El Acantilado, the award-winning and flagship restaurant owned by America's favorite chef and entrepreneur, Harrison Marshall, were everything. El Acantilado's patrons expected a unique and expensive dining experience. Kat was the first person to welcome them into the restaurant, and her first impression had to be favorable. Hence the designer dress, expertly applied makeup, glossy lips and black suede three-inch heels.

She was happiest in a pair of faded jeans and a T-shirt, her nearly waist-length hair in a ponytail or a braid and her face makeup-free, but this job paid the bills. If dressing up like a fashion model was what was required, she'd do it.

Kat tapped her pen against her leather-bound reservations book and looked into the wood-and-steel restaurant to watch the waitstaff. The newest waiter, Fred, seemed stressed, his hand wobbling as he placed Harrison's iconic roasted duck between the solid silver cutlery in front of Senator Cordell. Thank goodness he wasn't serving Elana Marshall, Harrison's daughter, who was sitting at the best table in the house with Jarrod Jones.

Hmm, Elana wasn't dining with her long-term boyfriend Thom. Jarrod's wife, the feted Irish actress Finola, was also missing.

God, Kat could make a fortune selling celebrity gossip to tabloid newspapers. They'd made her offers before, promised her anonymity, and she'd desperately needed the money.

Kat sighed. Selling gossip would be an easy solution to her financial woes. Damn her integrity and self-respect.

Kat smiled as Fred walked passed Elana's table, his gaze sliding sideways. The waitstaff was expected to turn a blind eye, to not notice a damn thing, but Fred was young and a little starstruck. And, really, since Elana Marshall looked like the millions of bucks she was reputed to be worth in that barely there dress highlighting her cleavage, how could Fred not notice that impressive rack, that fabulous face and those pouty lips?

Hadn't Kat, when she'd first started as a waitress years ago, been equally impressed by the star power that lit up the room? She'd stuttered when she'd first spoken to Angel Morales, the hottest and most talented celebrity around. She'd blushed when the younger Windsor brother had thanked her, very nicely, for a wonderful dining experience. She'd nearly fainted when a table of Oscar nominees had left her a two-thousand-dollar tip.

After serving so many wealthy and famous people, she was no longer easily impressed, and that was why she'd been promoted to the position of hostess a year or so ago. Harrison Marshall had personally promoted her, his decision based, he'd told her, on her popularity with his well-heeled clients. She was polite and personable, but she didn't fawn or simper. His clients, Harrison had said, liked that. They, apparently, liked her.

Kat looked down at her book and then at her watch. The Henleys were late, but then, they always were. Jonas Halstead and guest would be arriving within five minutes, and he was always on time.

Kat idly wondered who Jonas would be with tonight. By her calculations, the blond pop sensation he'd been dating for the past three months had reached her sell-by date, and there would be another girl on his arm tonight. Jonas, the billionaire property developer specializing in hotels and casinos, was a repeat visitor to El Acantilado over the past year. He'd recently bought Cliff House and was renovating the iconic Santa Barbara hotel. Rumor had it that he'd out-negotiated Harrison Marshall for the property, which suggested that Halstead was a hell of a businessman…or a shark.

Kat sighed. Tough businessman or not, his was the world she wanted to be in. The one she'd been destined for. The one that still beckoned to her. But, at twenty-eight years old, she was still working here and the closest she'd come to the world of finance was to show billionaire businessmen like Jonas Halstead to his table.

God. How sad.

"Katrina."

Kat's head snapped up and she silently cursed

when she realized Jonas was standing in front of her, impeccably dressed in a black designer suit worn over a rain-gray, open-necked shirt. Her eyes traveled up, across a broad chest and wide shoulders, along a tanned neck, to a strong jaw covered with two-day-old stubble and a mouth that was slow to smile but still sexy. He had a long, straight nose and deep green eyes under strong brows. Rich, successful and hot.

He had the reputation for being a bit of a bastard, in business and in bed. That fact only dropped his sexy factor by a quarter of a percent.

"Mr. Halstead, welcome back to El Acantilado," Kat murmured, ignoring her jumping heart and squirrelly stomach. Yeah, he was built and so damn handsome, but geez, she wasn't a twenty-two-year-old waitress anymore.

"Call me Jonas."

It wasn't the first time he'd made the offer, but Kat had no intention of accepting. It wasn't professional to call him by his first name, and not doing so kept a very healthy distance between her and the Jonas Halsteads of the world. Like her ex-husband and like her father, rich guys in fancy suits were not to be trusted.

Then again, what man could be?

But it really annoyed Kat that Jonas did funny things to her stomach and made her heart jump.

Fast, furious sexual attraction had led to her falling in love with and marrying Wes, and since he'd ended up using her heart as a Ping-Pong ball, she didn't trust her pheromones' ability to pick men wisely.

But every time she saw Jonas, her libido loudly reminded her that she hadn't had sex in a very long time. Jonas Halstead would be damn good at sex. He'd had, it was said, a lot of practice.

But tonight he was here alone. "Is your guest not joining you tonight?"

Jonas placed his hands in the pockets of his suit pants. "Rowan will be joining me shortly."

Kat widened her eyes in surprise. He was dating Rowan Greenly? The actress had just separated from her very volatile husband after a domestic abuse charge, and the hot-tempered rock star had threatened to kill anyone who made a move on his wife.

"You're brave. I suggest you wear a bulletproof vest," Kat couldn't help murmuring, even though she knew she was being indiscreet. "Rock likes his guns."

Jonas frowned, confused. Then his austere face softened as he released a low chuckle.

A thousand sparks danced on her skin as his smile turned his face from remote-but-still-hot to oh-my-God-I-want-to-rip-his-clothes-off. Kat placed her fist under her sternum and resisted the urge to scrunch her eyes shut.

No. God, no. She couldn't have the screaming hots for Jonas Halstead. She'd married, and divorced, a ruthless and merciless man. A competitive and cutthroat billionaire should be the last person to interest her. She was avoiding the male species in general, and the hot and sexy ones in particular.

Jonas was not her type.

The front door to the restaurant pulled open and all six feet and five inches of the best basketball talent in the country stepped into the restaurant. Rowan Brady. God, of course it was.

Kat glanced at Jonas, who lifted one dark eyebrow. "My date."

Rowan joined them, clasping Jonas's shoulder as he did. "Joe, we've known each other since we were kids and I keep telling you you're not my type."

Kat heard the teasing note in Rowan's deep voice and blushed as his dark eyes settled on her face. "And I'm curious as to why you'd want this gorgeous creature to think that I am."

Jonas slid Rowan a droll look. "Katrina thought I was meeting Rowan Greenly."

Rowan shuddered. "You have more sense than that. She's hot but her husband is psycho."

Jonas pulled his hands from his pockets and placed his forearms on her counter, the fabric of his suit bunching around impressive biceps. Kat lifted an eyebrow of her own, annoyed that she could easily imagine pushing that jacket off his shoulders and down his arms, ripping that shirt apart to find out whether his skin was as hot as she imagined.

She swallowed a moan. It was time to do her job. "Let me take you to your table, Mr. Halstead."

"Since you felt comfortable enough to make assumptions about my love life, you should be comfortable enough to call me Jonas. Or Joe."

Kat walked around the podium and gestured to the already full dining room. She deliberately ignored his provoking statement and his friend's amused expression. "I've placed you by the window. It has the most wonderful view of the beach below. This way, gentlemen." Kat started the familiar walk into the restaurant, forcing her expression into one of calm serenity.

Please don't look at my ass, Kat thought as Jonas fell into step behind her. *Or, if you do, please like it.*

For God's sake, Katrina! What is wrong with you?

"You have a—"

Thankful they were at his table, Kat turned and waited for his cocky comment.

But Jonas said nothing. He just moved to stand behind her, his height and width dwarfing her. He lifted his hand to her neck and Kat felt the tips of his fingers graze her skin. He barely made contact but suddenly her feet were glued to the floor and every cell in her body was set to vibrate. If he kissed her she'd spontaneously combust. She was sure of it.

Jonas twisted his hand and quickly snapped off the tag to her dress and held it up. "You obviously forgot to take it off. Here you go."

Kat's eyes bounced between the tag in his hand and his eyes, horror smothering the burning attraction she felt for the man.

Oh, crap, oh, crap, oh, crap. He'd ripped the tag when he pulled it off and she wouldn't be able to reattach it.

Oh, God, Tess had made it very clear that the bar code had to remain intact, that it could not be reproduced. Kat wouldn't be able to return the dress.

Her stomach climbed up her throat and lodged behind her tonsils. She was quite certain the air in the room was fast disappearing.

"Are you okay?" Jonas asked from a place far away. "Katrina?"

His voice pulled her back from the abyss, just a foot or so, enough for her to get some air into her lungs and oxygen to her brain.

You can't faint. You can't yell at him. You can't even react.

You need this damn job.

But she couldn't speak. She was unable to command her tongue to form even the smallest response. Intellectually she knew he thought he'd been doing her a favor, but his assumption had just piled another suitcase of stress onto the load she was already struggling to carry. Was this the straw that would break her back?

Kat suspected it might be. She snatched the tag from Jonas's hand and spun on her heel, praying she made it to the staff restroom without throwing up.

She now owed more than a thousand dollars on a dress she couldn't afford and it was Jonas Halstead's fault.

God, sexy man or not, if he had been eating with Rowan Greenly, Kat would have called Rowan's psycho husband and told him where to find Jonas.

And she would have suggested he bring his biggest gun.

Two

Kat, reaching her desk at the entrance of the restaurant and its adjoining bar, looked at the rows of liquor above the bartender's head and wished she could order something long, strong and alcoholic. Her eyes danced across a group in the corner, a girl and four guys, all pierced and tattooed. They were drinking the Mariella, the world-famous cocktail named after Harrison's wife. She could do with a Mariella, or three, right now. Actually she could really do with one of Mariella Santiago-Marshall's limitless, solid black credit cards or access to her bank account.

Crap. What the hell was she going to *do*?

"Please, *please* tell me you'd left the tag on the dress as a mistake—that you weren't planning on returning it in the morning."

Kat spun around and blinked at the multicolored creature standing in front of her. Her dress was a slinky cocktail number with a plunging neck and spaghetti straps the color of lemon sorbet. It was the perfect foil for the ink on her body. Pulling her eyes up from the amazing artwork, Kat looked into an elfin face dominated by a pair of warm brown eyes. The woman had a series of piercings in her lower lip and along her eyebrow; she had a tiny butterfly tattoo on her temple.

"You look amazing," Kat said. She sighed. It was obviously her night for allowing her mouth to run away with her.

"Thank you. But you didn't answer my question. Were you returning the dress?"

Kat looked into the restaurant and scowled in Halstead's direction. She never discussed one customer with another, but this woman would join her equally inked friends in the bar—birds of a feather—and she didn't see the harm in answering her question. Kat could spot a trust-fund baby at sixty paces and this woman was not one of them.

She lowered her voice. "Yes, it's borrowed. I was returning it in the morning. Now I'm going to have to pay for it, which was never the damned plan." Not sure what it was about this painted fairy that had her spilling her secrets, Kat continued, "God, I could just kill him. I don't have a thousand dollars to spend on a dress! I don't have a thousand dollars, full stop!"

"Thirteen hundred." The girl bit her lip. "It's a Callisto. Thirteen ninety-five, including tax."

Kat resisted the urge to bang her head against her desk. She swore, softly. “Dammit. I swear, I don’t care that he’s as sexy as sin and hotter than the sun, he’s a stupid, idiot man!”

Before the painted fairy could reply, Elana Marshall interrupted their conversation by placing a hand on Kat’s shoulder.

Kat spun around and smiled at the youngest Marshall and prayed that Elana hadn’t heard her last emphatic statement. “Hi, Elana, did you have a nice evening?”

The dimple in Elana’s cheek flashed. “I did. Thanks, Kat.”

Elana looked at Pixie Girl, her eyes bouncing from tat to tat, her mouth curving upward. “Love the angel on your arm.” Without waiting for a response, Elana turned her attention back to Kat. “So who is the idiot man?”

Kat wanted to scrunch her eyes shut in mortification. She and Elana were friends, sort of, in a “hey, how are you” sort of way. Elana was an heiress and Kat was Elana’s father’s employee. Kat’s eyes darted to Pixie Girl, silently begging her not to answer. She didn’t want Elana Marshall, who was the ultimate trust-fund baby, to know that her dress was on loan.

Pixie Girl smiled. “Aren’t they all, at one time or another?”

Elana nodded. “Pretty much. And here is one of mine.” Kat smiled at Elana’s date and thought that Elana could do a lot better than the married casting director. She could also do better than her fiancé,

Thom, who was really nice but…not for Elana. She needed someone with a personality as strong as hers.

But Kat had bigger problems to worry about than her boss's daughter's complicated love life. She had a job to do…a job she needed now more than ever.

Kat said good-night to Elana and turned back to the vision standing in front of her. "I am *so* sorry, you've been standing here forever. Let me walk you to the bar."

Pixie Girl grinned. "Actually, I'm joining Jonas Halstead's table."

Kat groaned and wondered if there was any way this night could get worse.

"Yeah," said Pixie Girl. "I'm meeting my boss and his friend for dinner."

"Please tell me that you work for Rowan Brady," Kat begged her.

She smiled, giving Kat a flash of her tongue stud. "Nope. I'm Sian and I work for Jonas Halstead."

Well, she had wondered whether this evening could get any worse.

Yep, Life answered her, *challenge accepted.*

The next morning, after a night long on worry and light on sleep, Kat heard the sound of a key in a lock. She brushed her hands across her wet cheekbones and rubbed her hands over her thighs, transferring her tears onto her old yoga pants. She heard the familiar thump of Tess's heavy bag hitting the floor and then her friend, with copper hair and freckles, stepped into Kat's small sitting area, holding—bless her—two cups of coffee.

"Yay, you're awake. I didn't know if you would be," Tess said, handing Kat a cup. "I got your text message this morning so I thought I'd pop in and see what the 'catastrophe' was." Tess sat next to Kat and peered into her face. "God, have you slept? At all?"

"I got home after midnight and I was too wound up for sleep." Not wanting to delay the bad news, she nodded at the designer dress lying over the chair. "I need to pay for the dress."

Tess's mouth dropped open. "Oh, crap, why?"

"Last night a guest, thinking he was being helpful, pulled the tag off," Kat told her, her voice flat. "The tag is toast."

Tess softly swore and wrinkled her nose. "Dammit, Kat, if you'd spilled something on it we could've had it cleaned. If it ripped, I would've had it mended, but I can't give a reasonable explanation as to why the label was ripped off."

Kat held up her hand. "I get it, Tess, I do. Stupid Jonas Halstead."

"The property mogul and one of California's hottest bachelors?" Tess's eyes widened. "He's an idiot for pulling the label off but, oh, my God, he's so sexy."

"He might be but he's put me in a hell of a position," Kat grumbled. "How soon do you need the money?"

Tess thought for a minute. "Miranda is away on vacation in Cancun for a month. So, basically, you have that long. And if you give me the money, I'll buy it and that way you'll get the staff discount. It's not much, only ten percent off, but it'll help."

Kat squeezed her knee. "Thanks, Tess." She rested her head on the back of her couch and closed her eyes.

"Or I can pay for it from my savings and you can pay me back," Tess added.

"Ah, Tess." It was a sweet offer. It didn't matter that Tess was her oldest friend. She couldn't accept her help. Thanks to her father and her ex-husband, Kat had massive issues around money. And trust.

It was easier, safer, cleaner, to go it alone.

Tess placed her coffee cup on the battered table with a thump. "You can't keep this up, Kat. You can't keep trying to do it all. You've even dropped weight. Are you eating?"

She ate at the restaurant most nights, with the chefs at the end of a shift. In between she lived on coffee and fresh air.

"Kat, something has got to change," Tess insisted, sitting on the edge of the seat.

"But what, Tess?" Kat demanded, resting her elbows on her knees. "The house June lives in is mine but my evil stepmom has the right to use it for the rest of her life and, in the terms of the will, I have to pay for the utilities and the upkeep. I have to carry the costs on a property I can't sell or use to get a loan."

"Why the hell didn't your dad leave you any cash?"

"Because he thought that, by the time he died,

I'd have a kick-ass, high-paying job. He also knew I had a rich husband to take care of me. He thought that if I couldn't pay for the house, Wes would pay for what I needed. I had someone to look after me. June did not."

"Your ex was such a psycho," Tess muttered, her expression dark.

Yep, beneath that charming all-American-boy exterior lived a sardonic, selfish narcissist who thought the sun disappeared when he sat.

"Okay, there's nothing you can do about the house but I don't understand why you are taking on the burden of Cath's medical bills," Tess stated, taking a sip of her coffee. She waved her hand. "I understand why you feel obliged to—when your mom died and your dad remarried Cruella, your aunt was there for you—but Cath is financially stable."

Kat pushed her hands into her hair. "She's really not, Tess. She has insurance but it's limited. Her cancer is rare and complicated and requires treatments her insurance doesn't cover. She's also paying for a full-time caregiver, which has wiped out the little disposable income she has." Kat shrugged. "So, between June's demands on the repairs to the house and sending cash Cath's way, I'm flat broke."

"Is she getting better?"

Kat felt her heart spasm as she shook her head. "I need her to see a specialist, but even if there wasn't a ridiculously long waiting list, they always seem to want money up front to cover the cost of her tests."

Kat rubbed the back of her neck and looked

around her small but cozy apartment. It was her favorite place in the world, a haven of color, the place where she could relax. After leaving the restaurant last night she'd returned home and spent a few hours crunching numbers on a spreadsheet.

One column held a list of expenses: rent, utility bills and food for herself; the repairs, maintenance and utility bills for the home her stepmom occupied; projected figures for Cath's medical expenses.

The other column, woefully small, held her income. There was a massive shortfall between the two amounts and she'd had yet to include paying for the damn dress.

God, how she wished she could roll back the years. She wished she hadn't taken a gap year between school and college to travel Europe. She wished she hadn't met and—in a haze of lust—married Wes. She'd managed to complete her degree in business administration, but there were lots of people with the same degree. She needed her MBA to earn the big bucks that would keep her head above water.

Over the past four years she'd managed to scrape together enough money to earn some credits toward her postgrad degree, but she still had a few courses to do. And she had to write her Leadership and Corporate Accountability exam in a few months. God knew when she was going to get time to study for that.

Yesterday she'd been treading water financially, but with a designer dress to pay for, she was now sinking below the surface. Tess was right. Something had to change, and fast. But what?

"I'm going to have to move," Kat reluctantly stated. "I'd save some money if I did. I can move back in with Cath."

Cath would love to have her and would refuse to charge her rent. If she did move back in, she could keep a better eye on Cath and monitor her health. But…damn, this apartment was her bolt-hole, her escape, the only place that was completely hers.

"This apartment block is owned by Harrison Marshall. Can't you ask the company to give you a break, to carry you for a month or two?" Tess asked.

Not possible. "They already give me a subsidy on my rent as part of my salary. I can't ask for more."

"So, essentially, you have a month to find the money to pay for the dress and to try to keep this apartment."

A month? God. "When you put it like that I want to bang my head against the wall," Kat muttered.

"Maybe something will come up. You never know."

"And I believe in unicorns and fairies…" Kat murmured, feeling utterly defeated. "God, Tess, for the first time ever, I'm totally out of ideas. What the hell am I going to do?"

Tess's eyes were full of compassion. "You're going to keep on believing that something amazing will happen. You're going to use your big brain and find a way because you are the smartest woman I know." Tess stood, took Kat's coffee from her hand and placed it on the coffee table. Pulling a throw off the single chair and then patting a pillow she placed against the arm of the sofa, she said, "But right now, you're going to sleep for a couple of hours."

"I've got stuff to do," Kat protested, her eyes heavy at just the mention of sleep.

"You need to decompress and you really need sleep," Tess insisted and watched as Kat curled her legs up onto the sofa and rested her head on the cushion. "You can't think straight without sleep, my darling. When you wake up, you'll feel so much better and you'll think of a solution."

God, she hoped so, Kat thought, closing her eyes. She was just about to drift off when she heard, once again, Tess's footsteps on her floor. "What did you lose, Tess?"

"Uh…it's not what I lost but what I found on your doorstep."

Hearing a note in Tess's voice that was a curious combination of both surprise and confusion, Kat forced her eyes open. She saw his feet first, trendy navy sneakers worn without socks. Indigo denim slacks covered muscular, long legs and a leather belt encircled a trim waist and what she suspected might be a washboard stomach. A striped blue-and-white shirt was tucked in and made his chest seem wider, his shoulders broader. The cuffs of his expensive shirt were rolled up to reveal tanned forearms and a Rolex encircling a strong wrist. His cotton shirt pulled tight across his big biceps and the collar of his shirt opened in a V to reveal a hint of his chest covered in a light dusting of hair.

Green, green eyes, messy hair, that sexy stubble

on his strong jaw. Man, what had she done to deserve Jonas Halstead standing in her apartment at 8:05 a.m.?

Kat slowly sat upright and frowned when she saw Tess backing away. Huh, so Tess wasn't sticking around for moral support. She frowned at her friend, who shrugged. "I have to get to work. I'm late as it is. Sorry," Tess explained, walking backward into the hall.

Sorry? She didn't look sorry at all. Kat slapped her bare feet onto the floor and stood, wishing she didn't look like a bag lady on a bad day. She ran her tongue over her teeth and pushed her hand into her hair, sighing when her hand snagged on a knot. Really? This was now her life?

Kat forced herself to meet Jonas Halstead's amused eyes. "What on earth are you doing here? How did you find me?"

He reached into the back pocket of his pants and tossed a check onto her coffee table. "Fourteen hundred dollars. It's to pay for the dress I ruined."

Bloody Sian. Kat had thought she'd keep her mouth shut! Dammit. Kat looked at the check, sighed and decided to lie her ass off. "I have no idea what you are talking about."

Jonas jammed his hands into the pockets of his pants and narrowed his eyes at her. "The hell you don't. You borrowed a designer dress. You were going to return it. I pulled the tag off, which, as Sian told me, was a stupid ass thing to do. You are now on the hook for fourteen hundred dollars. I'm taking you off the hook."

Kat looked at the check, back up to his determined face and back down to the check again. God, it was so tempting to take his money. It had been his fault. He had pulled the tag off and it wasn't like he couldn't afford the donation. He was Jonas Halstead, billionaire.

But it was still a donation and she didn't accept charity, ever. She especially didn't take handouts from sexy men who threw cash around like it was confetti. Nothing was simple when it came to money and motives should always be questioned. Nobody, especially hard-assed businessmen, handed out money without wanting something in return.

Between her ex and her father, she was sick of men and the games they played with money. Kat folded her arms across her chest and shook her head. "I'm not going to cash your check."

Shock ran across his face, through his eyes. "What?"

"I'm not taking your money." Kat spoke slowly, as if she were her explaining her position to a three-year-old. "I chose to wear the dress, even knowing that I couldn't afford to pay for it if something went wrong. Something did go wrong, but it's my problem, not yours."

"The hell it is!" Jonas snapped back, his green eyes flashing with frustration. "I should not have been presumptuous enough to take the tag off."

"Maybe not, but I'm still not taking your money," Kat told him, feeling stubborn.

"Consider it a tip," Jonas suggested, matching her bullishness with a healthy dose of his own.

"Too late for that," Kat said. "Thanks for the offer but…no."

"You are the most infuriating, annoying, frustrating, sexy…"

Kat hauled in a breath when he said the last word and their eyes clashed and held. One little word and something hot and crazy buzzed between them. The air around them seemed to thicken and tighten, filling with electricity. God, he was as attracted to her as she was to him. She saw it in the way he clenched and unclenched his fists, in the green fire in his eyes. If she took one step toward him she'd be in his arms. She'd feel the heat and strength of him. She would know whether his sexy lips felt as good as they looked, whether sparks would jump from her skin under the warmth of his hands.

She wanted him. Annoying, cash-on-the-table cretin that he was, she wanted to taste him, feel him, make love to him. She was losing her mind; she was sure of it. Too much stress and not enough sleep… this craziness was the result.

Kat heard Jonas snap out a swear word, heard his "This is insane" mutter. Then his hand breached the space between them and his fingers encircled her wrist. He held her lightly, giving her the opportunity to pull out of his grip if she so wanted.

She didn't.

Instead Kat allowed him to pull her in. She didn't step away when his hand rested on her lower back and jerked her hips into his, allowing her to feel the hard length of his erection pushing into her stomach. His other hand covered her right breast; his thumb finding her nipple with deadly accuracy. He hadn't even kissed her yet and her panties were damp.

If he didn't kiss her she would die. From want, need, sheer frustration. Kat stood on her tiptoes, her mouth aligned with his. Not bothering to be coy, she slammed her lips onto his, her tongue darting out to trace the seam, to tempt him to open up.

This wasn't her, Kat thought from a place far away. She waited for men to make the first move, to kiss her, to lead. She followed. But not today.

Jonas swiped her nipple with his thumb, held her tight against him and let her kiss him. When he didn't open his mouth or kiss her back, Kat, unsure of what she was doing or whether she should be doing this at all, started to pull away. Jonas growled a harsh *no* against her mouth and moved his hand from her breast to the back of her head to keep her in place. She wasn't going anywhere, Kat realized, and when his mouth started to move, she also realized she didn't want to.

Jonas Halstead was kissing her. It was candy floss and crack, sunshine and sin, pleasure and pain. He took command of her mouth, his tongue tangling with hers in a sexy dance. Kat, senseless, pulled his shirt from the back of his pants and put her hands on his hot, masculine skin. Jonas groaned his pleasure and she ran her palms over his gorgeous ass, annoyed at the barrier of clothes between her fingers and his flesh.

Jonas kissed the corner of her mouth and trailed his lips over her jaw, down her neck. It had been a long time since a man had kissed her liked this, touched her like she was something infinitely precious and incandescently gorgeous. She'd missed this. His teeth scraped across her collarbone. The tiny sting and the wave of pleasure made Kat's eyes fly open. Her gaze landed on the dress.

The one he'd just offered to pay for.

Kat stiffened in his arms as dismay swamped desire. Oh, God, did he think she was taking the money and this was her way of showing her gratitude? Did he think she was so easily manipulated? Did he think she was desperate, so eager to be with a man who was supposed to be brilliant at business? And in bed?

What the hell was wrong with her?

Kat jerked away from him and wrapped her hands around her waist.

"What did I do?"

Cynicism returned and Kat snorted, convinced he'd practiced that expression of puzzled surprise. "I'm not taking your check and, to be very clear, I'm not sleeping with you."

Jonas's eyes turned frosty. "I didn't make that assumption," he said, his soft voice holding an edge of danger. "And sex is not what I came for."

"Really?" Kat whipped out the words. "You didn't take very long to kiss me."

Jonas jammed his hands into the pockets of his

jeans, those clever lips now thin with anger. "I'd like to point out that you didn't fight me off." He pulled on the tail of his shirt before tucking it back into his pants. "This shirt didn't pull itself loose."

Kat blushed, dropped her eyes and released an irritated sigh.

"Why are you mad, Katrina? Because I kissed you or because you liked it and wanted me to do more?"

Neither. Both. *Crap.*

Kat, feeling thoroughly off balance, brushed past him, deliberately connecting her shoulder with the top of his bicep before storming toward the hallway. Her attempt at intimidation had as much impact as a fly trying to move a cow.

When she reached her front door, she pulled it open and, when Jonas reached her, she gestured for him to keep on walking. "Just go."

"No. You're obviously upset and I want to know why."

She could never explain. For the first time in four years, for a few minutes in his arms, she'd felt protected, not so alone. She'd felt like the world wasn't conspiring against her, that life would get better, that things would eventually be okay. It had nothing to do with the check but everything to do with his strength, the power that radiated from him. He made her feel stronger…

God, he made her want to lean, to ask for help, to think that maybe, someday, she could trust someone again. Love someone again. He made her remember what attraction and pleasure and, dammit, what affection felt like. She'd deliberately pushed all of that away, locked all those emotions and memories in a box, refusing to look at them. Memories hurt, dammit.

But one kiss from Halstead had snapped that lock like it was made of spun sugar. She couldn't allow herself to look back; she couldn't afford to remember. It hurt too damn much. And, worse, it might tempt her to make the same mistakes she had before.

"Please go."

"Katrina..."

Kat was quite convinced that her head was one minute away from exploding. Anger rolled in—so much easier to deal with than fear. "My name," she yelled, "is Kat! I'm twenty-eight years old. I haven't had sex in four years. I'm flat broke and I've done no work to prepare for my LCA final! I'm exhausted and I don't need this! I have exactly one nerve left and you're friggin' standing on it. Go away!"

Kat felt her lungs pumping, heard the buzzing in her head and knew that if he attempted to speak again, she would kill him. Slowly. With her bare hands. It didn't matter that he was twice her size, she had so much adrenaline and unused sexual energy pumping around her system that she could take on a herd of angry hippos and win. Jonas Halstead didn't have a chance in hell.

Jonas sent her a you're-bat-crap-crazy look and walked into the hallway.

Kat slammed the door closed behind him and stomped through her living room into her bedroom.

Climbing into bed, she pulled the covers over her head and wished she could just stay there for the rest of her life.

Because, dammit, Jonas Halstead's check was still on her coffee table. And because she was now, more than ever, tempted to cash it.

Three

Jonas looked up when Sian walked into his office and slammed the door behind her. He lifted his eyebrows, leaned back in his chair and waited for her to offload. He knew, from experience, that it wouldn't take long.

She went into all they had to do in their temporary office in Santa Barbara. The builders at Cliff House had found mold in the basement, the masons rebuilding the stone walkways were behind schedule and the anchor tenant destined for their new mall in Austin, Texas, now had cold feet. The investors for a ski resort in Whistler were uneasy—global downturn, less disposable income, global warming—and their head of human resources was moving to the East Coast.

Yet all Jonas could think about was the hot kiss

he'd shared with Katrina—Kat—and the fact that she had yet to cash his check. Damned stubborn woman.

Walking away from her instead of taking her where they'd stood had required every bit of self-control he'd possessed. He'd never become so lost in a kiss, so carried away in a woman's arms. He'd loved kissing her, touching her, and would have loved to have done more.

So much more.

That was all well and good but he didn't like the fact that Kat Morrison, hostess at the best restaurant in Santa Barbara—flat broke and currently celibate—had the ability to make him forget his own name.

He didn't like that at all.

But he couldn't stop thinking about her, remembering how soft her skin had felt under his hands, the spice of her mouth, those breathy sounds she'd made in the back of her throat. And her smell, something clean and natural, seemed lodged in his nose. He was also—and this was worrying—curious and, worse, concerned about her. She had a good job, why was she broke? Why didn't she have a boyfriend? She'd mentioned an LCA final and, as he remembered from his college days, that stood for Leadership and Corporate Accountability—part of the MBA program. He could handle her beauty and her sex appeal but if she was as bright as he suspected, he was in big trouble.

There was nothing more dangerous than a gorgeous, brainy woman.

Sian's small hand slapped his desk and he snapped back to the present. Talking about brainy, sexy women, this one was looking vastly irritated. "Will you please concentrate?"

Jonas nodded and quickly issued a list of instructions to, hopefully, address all the issues she'd raised. "Did I get them all?" he asked.

Sian nodded. "That is so annoying, especially since I didn't have your full attention."

"I can multitask."

Sian threw her pen down and linked her hands around her knee. "Want to tell me what's going on with you? And don't tell me nothing—you've been acting like a bear for the last two weeks."

"Jack," Jonas stated, making his grandfather's name sound like a curse.

"Oh, dear." Sian stood, walked over to the small fridge in the corner of the room and pulled out two ice waters. She handed one to Jonas, who cracked the lid for her before taking the unopened bottle for himself.

"So, what did the old buzzard do this time?"

"He told me I have three months—two and three-quarter months now—to marry or else he is disinheriting me."

Sian smiled, thinking he was joking. When he held her gaze, her mouth opened in shock. "You have got to be kidding me!"

"I so wish I was," Jonas replied. He'd spent the past week trying to convince himself that Jack wasn't being serious, that he was jerking Jonas around, but then Preston had sent him an official letter stating his client's position and assuring Jonas that his grandfather was deadly serious about him finding a wife.

Jonas had to marry or he'd lose everything he'd worked for, everything that made sense to him. He felt the burn of a rumbling ulcer and took another sip of water.

And even if he hadn't received a letter from Preston, he would've sensed Jack's displeasure from the cold telephone conversations they'd shared since that breakfast, Jack's terse and snappy emails. When circumstances went his way, his grandfather was congenial and charming, occasionally affectionate. When he was thwarted, he grew arctic cold and withdrew. Trying to stay on Jack's good side was like trying to herd cats, futile and exhausting.

After five minutes of thoughtful silence, Sian lifted a shoulder and the scales of the inked dragon covering her skin rippled. "Well, it seems like you don't have a hell of a lot of choice," Sian said. "Marry someone."

"Okay, pencil it in my diary and I'll meet you at the courthouse."

Sian's laughter danced on the sunlight. "Ha, ha, funny man. Garth has been asking me to marry him for a year and I keep telling him hell, no! So the chances of me marrying someone I don't love, even you, are less than zero. Besides, if you married me, Jack would definitely disinherit you."

Jack, narrow-minded as he was, couldn't look past the tattoos to see the razor-sharp brain Sian possessed. "Crap, Si, what the hell am I going to do? I need a wife. Where will I find someone to marry before the deadline? Maybe if I grovel, Gigi would take me back."

Sian shuddered. "You wouldn't need to grovel, you'd just need to crook your finger in her direction and she'd come skipping back. No! I absolutely refuse to let you do that. You'll be divorced within six months."

And why would that be a problem? If he went through with this crazy scheme, he intended to be married to his temporary bride for the least amount of time possible.

Sian stood and walked around so that she sat on the corner of his desk, facing him. "C'mon, Joe, there's got to be someone else you've met lately who would be a better bet than that whiny, vain actress."

Katrina's face immediately popped into his head.

"You're thinking of someone." Sian pushed a finger into his chest. "Tell me! Who?"

Jonas shook his head, sending a glance at his monitor. "Nobody. C'mon, Si, back to work."

Sian crossed her arms and glared at him. "No. Tell me who you are thinking of."

He felt like he was ten years old and had been caught with his hand in the cookie jar. "It wouldn't work. We're too different."

"Jonas! Who?"

"Kat. Katrina Morrison," Jonas finally admitted, meeting her eyes and daring her to laugh at him. Hell, he wouldn't blame her if she did. If he wasn't feeling so damn morose and confused and terrified, he'd be laughing, too.

But Sian just cocked her head and slowly nodded. "Yeah, I could see you marrying her. She's really nice and, despite only meeting her once, I really like her. You'd also, might I point this out, make spectacular babies."

Jonas felt like she was gripping his windpipe and squeezing. "Okay, let's get one thing straight, I am not looking for a wife."

Sian lifted a thin, cocky eyebrow. "I'm sorry, did I misunderstand you? Didn't you just say… 'I need a wife'?"

"A temporary wife. A pretend wife. Not a *wife* wife," Jonas snapped.

"*Wife* wife?"

This conversation was getting ridiculous. Jonas gripped the bridge of his nose, trying to control his temper. Sian was treading on dangerous ground, teasing him about this. "I plan on keeping her around long enough to satisfy my grandfather. As soon as I get the company shares transferred to me, she's out of my life."

A small frown appeared between Sian's eyebrows. "Isn't that a bit calculating?"

"Hey, I didn't make the rules. I'm just playing the game!" Jonas retorted. "I want a woman I can stand being around for less than a year, someone who doesn't think this is forever. But I don't want a gold digger."

"Talking of…did you see the three-page spread in *People*? Sara is divorcing husband number five—"

"Remind me, husband number five is the Hollywood director?" The tabloid press was how he kept tabs on his mother, and Jonas liked it that way. Actually, he'd prefer it if Sian didn't even tell him what she read, but she liked to torture him.

"Yep. Apparently she's having an affair with Mervin Kline."

Sara, so faithful.

"Kline is said to be the tenth richest man in the country…"

"Ah." Now Sara's actions made sense. Her main ambition, Jonas was sure, was to be the wife of the richest man in the world. His father, Sara's first husband, had just been a practice run. She hadn't even stuck around long enough for him to be a practice child. She'd just bailed, saying that motherhood wasn't her thing. Seducing and then marrying rich men—that's where her talents lay.

It shouldn't hurt that the last time he'd spoken to her was when he'd turned thirty, five years ago. He'd called her on his birthday, not the other way around. Jonas was pretty sure she'd wiped the memory of giving birth from her mind. After all, you couldn't say you were in your early forties when you had a son in his midthirties.

"We need to get back to work, Sian, so get off my desk."

"Oh, touchy." Sian saw something in his face and she winced. She held up her hand, her expression requesting his patience. "Why don't you ask Kat out to dinner, see if you like her enough to temporarily marry her?"

He couldn't get Kat to cash his check. She'd yelled at him after they'd kissed. She was a basket of complicated. She had issues, and Jonas tried, whenever possible, to avoid issues. He needed this search for a wife to be complication-free, easy, businesslike. An emotion-free zone.

Kat was independent, mouthy, annoying—sheer hard work. She was trouble. He should be running from her as fast as he could. She was the last person he should marry.

But he thought that, probably, he was going to anyway.

Sian, reading his mind, patted his arm. "Good luck, boss."

He was going to need it. Jonas rose and bent to drop a kiss on her cheek, grateful that he had her in his life, standing in his corner. He rested his forehead on hers. "Are you sure you won't marry me?"

Sian patted his cheek. "Darling, not even for you."

Kat was glad for the madness of Friday lunch service. It kept her from worrying about Cath, from thinking about her money problems and the fact that she was going to have to leave her beloved apartment.

But mostly, being busy kept her from thinking about Jonas Halstead and how she'd felt in his arms. Kat stared down at her reservations book and tried to concentrate on who she would seat where. She had reservations for both the current and ex-wife of a famous producer, former best friends, and, in the interest of peace, she needed to keep them on opposite sides of the restaurant and out of each other's sight…

Kat's thoughts wandered back to Jonas.

He knew exactly how to kiss her, how much pressure to apply to her nipple with his thumb. His kisses had been pure magic… He was all heat and power. Six foot two of pure masculinity. Broad-shouldered, muscled, powerful, he just had to look at her with heat in those smoky green eyes and she felt the urge to strip and climb all over him.

What the hell was wrong with her? Okay, sure, she'd been celibate for a while, but she wasn't the type to go all dizzy over a man. With the few lovers she'd had and even with Wes, getting naked had required a mental shift, a deliberate decision. With Halstead, her much-neglected libido had been calling the shots. Her body wanted to be against his, skin to skin.

Why him? Why now?

And why couldn't she get him out of her head?

Kat glanced at her watch, saw that she had another ten minutes before the restaurant was due to open and mentally allocated clients to tables, trying to keep her mind on her much-needed job. It wasn't as if she would see him again anytime soon!

Unless he came back here.

Crap! Kat bit her lip and quickly flipped through the reservations book. She hadn't booked a table for

Jonas, but she was one of four hosts and he could've spoken to any of the others. Kat ran through the reservations for the next month and didn't see his name, but she knew there were many women who'd booked a table for themselves and a "guest." It wasn't an impossibility that Halstead could be a dinner companion. A model, an actress, the lead singer of an indie pop group—these women were his type. Actually, Kat suspected that any woman breathing was his type. Halstead made no bones about his disinterest in settling down.

On that score, Kat couldn't fault him. Marriage and commitment were games for fools and she'd never play again. Wes had ruined vows for her and ruined them well. She'd gone into their marriage in a starry-eyed haze, flying on a magic carpet of attention and compliments. The sex hadn't been great, but having someone so solidly in her corner, so deeply supportive, had more than made up for the infrequent, fumbling, lets-do-it-with-the-lights-off sex.

Their sex life would get better after they were married, she'd told herself. She'd been wrong. Nothing improved. In fact, everything had started sliding downhill a scant week after they'd returned from their two-week honeymoon. They might be married, Wes had informed her, but he had no intention of carrying her, financially or emotionally, anymore. He expected her to pull her weight.

Since she was now living with him, he'd said, all expenses were to be split equally. The fact that she was a full-time student and he had a corporate position held no bearing on the situation. She believed in women's rights, didn't she? Well, it was time to stand by her principles.

Not recognizing the man she'd married, and determined to keep up the pretense of being happy, Kat had taken two part-time jobs to cover her financial obligations, thinking that one day soon things would improve. They were getting used to each other, she'd thought. Everyone said the first year of marriage was the hardest.

Then her father had died. Six months later she was divorced and one month after that Cath was diagnosed. Kat's world fell to pieces.

Her dysfunctional marriage—and her father ignoring her in his will—created a pit inside where cynicism flourished. Kat was unable to trust a person's words, knowing actions were what counted. No, it was better to be independent, to sort out her own problems, to do it herself. That way no one could disappoint her and no one could hurt her.

But, damn, Jonas reminded her that she could really do with some hot, messy sex. A man's hard body on hers, strong fingers pressing into her flesh, masculine lips kissing her lips and throat and heading lower to suck her nipples, to make tracks over her stomach, to—

"Hey, Kat, are you going to open? It's time."

Kat jerked her head up and snapped out of her daydream, embarrassed that she was fantasizing about Jonas Halstead at work. God, this had to stop, she thought, walking over to the front door to slide it open. Jonas was out of her league. He was a billionaire and she was a restaurant hostess, someone who was only noticed when things went wrong.

Besides, he'd forgotten about her already. He'd handed her a check, appeased his conscience and moved on to his next blonde. It was time she moved on, too…

Kat put her shoulder to the heavy wood-and-glass door and frowned when it easily slid on its track. She felt the heat of a masculine body behind her, inhaled the scent of lime and sandalwood from an expensive cologne and looked up to see a strong hand on the frame above her head, cuffs rolled back and a Rolex watch she immediately recognized.

"Hello, Kat."

Kat leaned her forehead against the wooden frame of the door and counted to ten and then to twenty. Jonas was back. He didn't have a reservation, so the only reason he could be there was to see her.

What could he want? Kat stood straight, turned around and looked at the man who'd invaded her dreams over the last ten days or so.

"What do you want, Mr. Halstead?"

The corners of this mouth tipped up at her formal tone. "God, I love that prissy voice of yours."

Kat didn't know how to respond so she just folded her arms and tapped her foot.

"Are you working tonight? Would you like to have dinner with me?"

"I'm not working," Kat replied, walking back to her hostess's desk. Scooting behind it, she reached into the narrow cupboard and yanked out her bag. Opening the zip, she removed an envelope.

"Okay, so I'll collect you at seven thirty," Jonas said, supremely confident.

"I might be free, but I'm not going to dinner with you," Kat told him, wishing she was brave enough, bold enough, to tell him she didn't want food but she wouldn't say no to a night of no-strings, blow-her-socks-off sex. But she'd never been a girl who could so frankly state what she wanted.

Besides, as hot as that fantasy was, she wasn't really the one-night-stand type.

"Why not?" Jonas demanded, frowning.

Kat looked at him, amused by the confusion on his face. Obviously he didn't hear the word *no* very often, and why would he? He was good-looking, rich, successful and smart. When he asked a woman out, the default response was probably "Yes, yes, God, yes."

But for Kat, there were so many reasons to say no. *I don't have time to date. You're so out of my league. We have nothing in common. But, mostly, I hate that I'm so crazy attracted to you that there's a good chance I'll jump you as soon as we're alone.*

Unable to tell him the truth, Kat used an old standby. "I'm not allowed to fraternize with clients, Mr. Halstead. I could lose my job and my job is very, very important to me." It wasn't a big lie. Dating clients wasn't encouraged, but neither was it forbidden.

"Because you're flat broke."

Damn him for remembering that! "I need the

money, yes. Most normal people do need a salary to keep the wolf from the door," Kat replied, her tone implying that he had no concept of what it felt like to live from hand to mouth.

"If you're in such dire need of cash, then why didn't you cash my check?" Jonas demanded. "After all, it's not like I'd miss fourteen hundred dollars."

"I don't take charity, Mr. Halstead. Not even from rich, smug billionaires."

Kat handed the envelope to him and watched as he took it, the paper white against his tanned hand.

Jonas slid his finger under the flap, lifted it and frowned when he saw the contents. She'd cut the check into pieces as small as confetti and she'd planned to post the envelope to him, care of the Halstead & Sons head offices in Santa Monica. Seeing his annoyance in person was so much more satisfying.

"Did you enjoy doing that?" Jonas asked, his tone bland and his expression now inscrutable.

"I did," Kat admitted.

Jonas tucked the envelope into the back pocket of his stone-colored slacks and nodded once. A small smile hovered around his lips. "Are you sure you don't want to have dinner?"

"I'm sure," Kat said, trying not to look at his mouth and failing.

"Your mouth is spouting one thing but your eyes are telling me you wouldn't mind getting naked and crawling all over me."

God! This man! His ego! But was it ego when he was telling the truth?

Kat, feeling flushed, deliberately looked at her watch, a knockoff Tag she'd bought off a street vendor. Then she sent him a glance meant to stop him in his tracks. "You've wasted enough of my time, Mr. Halstead. I'm sure you've got better things to do."

Jonas shrugged, the muscles of his shoulders rippling under his white dress shirt. "Not really. But I'll let you go."

Kat rolled her eyes. "You speak as if you can stop me."

Jonas's eyes dropped to her mouth, to her breasts and back up again. He stepped toward her and raised his hand, cupping the side of her face. He stared down at her, his green eyes cutting through her bravado.

"Katrina, we both know that if I kissed you right now, you wouldn't know your name in ten seconds."

Before she could stutter a response, Jonas dropped his head and oh, so gently kissed the corner of her mouth.

A rush of electricity skittered through her body. Damn the man.

Jonas stepped back and tapped her nose with his finger before walking out of the restaurant and down the flight of stairs to the circular driveway. Kat watched as he walked toward his SUV. She'd expected him to drive a low-slung sports car, something flashy, but the expensive SUV was a surprise. It was more down-to-earth than she'd expected.

Well, huh. Kat bit her lip, her fingers lifting to her mouth, where she could still feel the imprint of that sexy kiss. He was right, damn him. If he had kissed her, she would've forgotten her name in seconds.

And that annoyed the hell out of her.

It had been a long, frustrating day and Jonas knew he had two choices. He could throttle the next person who screwed up or he could go for a run. He decided to take his bad mood to the streets of Santa Barbara.

He'd been too busy to explore the town since he'd arrived. He was staying at a boutique hotel in the heart of downtown and he made his way to State Street, mentally running through the directions the manager had given him. After doing a few stretches, he started to run, cruising past the eclectic shops, artsy cafés and small theaters.

This was Harrison Marshall's town, he thought. Harrison, his friend and competitor, was a local boy, but he hadn't come from the same income bracket as his highborn wife. Harrison had scrambled for everything he had and Jonas rather liked that about the man. Jonas hadn't had to struggle but, unbeknownst to many people, Jack hadn't made it easy for his grandson to take over the company.

During Jonas's vacations from college, Jack had put him to work as a low-paid laborer, doing whatever grunt work the site manager needed. When Jonas graduated college with a business degree, he'd spent years proving himself to Jack. After spending time in supply chain management, human resources and project management, he'd been promoted to vice president. He'd worked directly under his father, who'd been the chief financial officer at the time. Those six months had been pure torture. Jonas had realized Halstead only had space for one of them, and after a life-changing fight, he'd stayed and Lane had left.

He'd taken over from Lane as CFO and then secured the job as Halstead & Sons' CEO. And, even if he said so himself, he was doing a damn good job.

Of course, he'd worked insane hours to grow the company, but Jack still wasn't satisfied. His grandfather still wanted another few pints of Jonas's blood, another ten pounds of his flesh.

Damned Jack. He'd only be content when Jonas was married and Jack was dangling the next generation of Halsteads on his knee. But, knowing Jack and his demand for perfection, he might not be satisfied even then. It seemed to Jonas that whenever he reached one goal, Jack moved the finishing line. No matter how hard he worked, Jonas would never fulfil Jack's expectations.

He wanted to draw his own damn line, march to the beat of his own drum, be judged on his own merits. He wanted to stand apart from Jack. He wanted his company, his family name, to be one his investors trusted. He wanted to prove he could make tough calls while avoiding the dodgy business practices his father had engaged in. Jonas wanted to do it his way, the *right* way.

But to do it his way he had to marry.

Jonas ran under the freeway overpass, crossed over a bridge and soon saw the Dolphin Fountain and, beyond it, the wide beach. He took a moment to watch the sea. He liked this town. He decided to run to the end of Stearns Wharf instead of along the beach. His feet slapped against the pier as he watched the anglers and sailors unload their gear. At the top of the pier he headed back and wondered if Kat ever came down here. Did she walk or run this route?

Kat. He frowned, remembering his shredded check. Why hadn't she cashed it to pay for the dress? It made no sense to him. She needed the money and it was his fault she now owed so much since he was the one who'd ripped off the tag. It wasn't like he'd miss the cash.

But she'd still refused. And, damn, that made him respect her. He couldn't remember when a woman had last refused his offer to pay for anything. Whether it was dinner or drinks or a cab or a handbag they fancied—one woman he'd dated had asked him to pay for silicon butt implants, for God's sake—he was their access to easy cash. Sometimes he handed over his card, most times he didn't. He simply could not recall a woman passing up a chance to spend his money.

Neither could he remember when a woman had refused to have dinner with him, when one had brushed him off. Kat's reaction was definitely a first. In the world of dating and casual hookups, in the world of getting what you want with the least amount of effort, Kat was…well, a freak.

She didn't play by the rules. Hell, she wasn't playing at all. She was an unknown quantity. And that had to change. Seeing a bench ahead of him, Jonas slowed and then stopped. He pulled his cell phone from the pouch on his arm and found the number he was looking for.

"Jonas Halstead, you bastard."

Jonas grinned at the familiar voice. So Harrison still hadn't forgiven him for stealing Cliff House out from under his nose. Harrison thought he'd had the deal sewed up. No deal, as Jack frequently reminded Jonas, was concluded until the ink on the signatures was dry.

"Since I've known you so long, I thought you might've had the decency to keep your hands off my deals."

Jonas grinned. "Would you have tried to steal it from me?"

"Damn right!" Harrison readily admitted, laughter in his voice. "So, my friend, what can I do for you?"

"Katrina Morrison," Jonas stated.

Jonas heard his swift intake of breath. "I can cope with you stealing the Cliff House but I will be super pissed if you steal my best hostess, Jonas."

"Relax," Jonas told him. "I'm not going to steal her." Not that it was a bad idea. "Not today, at least."

He heard Harrison's growl and grinned.

"Why do you want to know about Kat? You interested in her?"

"Maybe."

"Don't bother, son. I keep an eye and ear on key

staff at my restaurants and Kat has refused offers ranging from dinners to apartments from a variety of men."

"She says it's against company policy."

Harrison was quiet for a few beats. "Kat knows that if she met a man at El Acantilado, I'd trust her to keep her work and personal life separate. She's just not interested, as far as I know."

"She's young and gorgeous, why not?"

"No idea. All I know is that she's a hard worker and she has some money issues. She's not as tough as she looks. If you cause her any pain, I will not be pleased."

Harrison spoke in a flat, don't-doubt-me voice Jonas was unaccustomed to hearing from him. He was obviously protective of Katrina. Since Harrison had the habit of meddling in his friends', family's and employees' lives, Jonas wondered why he hadn't waved his magic wand and sorted out whatever was troubling Kat. Rumors swirled about just how far Harrison's reach went. He'd supposedly squashed negative reports around a friend's daughter's drunken rampage in Cancun, kept a chef out of jail and saved a good friend from a revengeful mistress. Helping Kat shouldn't have been a problem.

Curious, Jonas asked him for an explanation.

"She won't let me," Harrison grumbled. "She's the most independent, stubborn woman I've ever met. She's determined to sort out her own life in her own way and she consistently refuses my help."

"So annoying when they do that," Jonas murmured, amused that Kat had the guts to refuse one of the wealthiest and most powerful men in California. Amused and, despite himself, impressed.

"All Kat will accept from me is a discount on her rent since I own her apartment block. Though I hear she's leaving at the end of the month because she can't make the rent, something about an unexpected expense that sideswiped her."

That damned dress.

Even as he scowled, he realized her independence was attractive. Since she was so determined to go it alone, she would be the perfect wife, not interested in his money or what she could get from him. Maybe they could strike a deal.

But an out-of-the-blue marriage proposal wasn't something he could dump on a stranger. He'd need to establish some sort of relationship with her first. A friendship at the very least. While he did that, he had to keep his hands off her. Their blistering sexual attraction was a complication…for now.

But if they were to be married for ten months, a year, that attraction could be a fun way to pass the time.

"If she's got money issues then I'll cover her rent for the next few months," Jonas told Harrison.

"Even if I allowed you to do that, she won't accept any charity," Harrison told him.

"Tell her that it's another raise. She needs the job, so she'll listen to you," Jonas insisted. "Come on, Harrison…"

"Are you going to hurt her?" Harrison asked, his tone full of doubt.

"Believe it or not, I'm trying to help her," Jonas told him and it was true. He needed a wife; Kat needed money.

Harrison agreed to offer Kat's rent as a salary increase, told Jonas he'd eviscerate him if he messed with Kat and Jonas responded by thanking Harrison before disconnecting the call. He placed his phone back into the pouch on his arm and started to jog again.

It would take some quick and smart work to get what he wanted, but that was okay. He was smart and hard work didn't scare him.

He was definitely going to marry Katrina Morrison, Jonas thought, grinning.

God help them both.

Four

It was past midnight. Kat had worked a double shift and she was so tired she wanted to cry. Harrison Marshall had run the kitchen tonight and his wife, Mariella, had also been in-house. She was joined by her nephew Gabe, who was their right-hand man and, Kat suspected, somewhat of a power behind the Marshall throne. The presence of the Marshalls changed the atmosphere within the walls of the establishment; it ramped up the staff and put them on edge. Kat included.

As a result, by the end of her double shift, Kat had a tension headache that threatened to split her skull open. Slipping out the back exit of the restaurant, she headed for the staff parking lot, her feet aching.

Kat stopped to pull off her three-inch heels. Opening her bag, she looked for the pair of flips-flops she routinely carried for moments like these. Dammit, she must have left them at home. Well, she could either walk to her car in her bare feet or slip her heels back on. Squeezing her feet back inside those shoes would hurt like hell, so Kat walked across the swath of lawn barefoot, enjoying the feel of the cool grass between her toes.

Kat heard stones rattle and looked up to see the outline of a big man leaning against the hood of her small car. She should be scared. His face was in shadow and he looked menacing. But she wasn't scared. Thanks to her thumping heart and her tingling skin, she immediately recognized Jonas. He was waiting for her. Why?

Kat slowly walked toward her car, desperately trying to ignore the little voice inside reminding her how good it felt to have someone waiting for her and even better that he was big and brawny and oh, so sexy.

She stepped off the grass and picked her way over to her car. Ignoring Jonas, she opened the passenger-side door, tossed her bag and heels onto the seat and slammed the door to the rust-bucket car closed.

"Hi, stalker," she drawled as she walked around the car to the driver's door.

"Hi back."

Kat tipped her head to the side. "Why are you here?"

"I was thinking about you and the next thing I

found myself here, waiting for you. It's utterly bizarre."

Of course it was bizarre because she was the last woman in the world he should be interested in. Like most rich, single men—and married men who thought they were single—he had a type. She'd seen his type over these past few months: gorgeous and easily able to navigate the world he lived in.

Jonas was only interested in her because she'd turned him down. Kat knew people craved what was just out of their reach. He could buy anything he wanted. He snapped his fingers and people jumped. Her refusal to date him was a novelty, made more exciting because she'd said no. He wanted to be the guy to wear her down, to have what he thought others could not. She was his goal and he didn't give up easily.

She had no time or energy to play his games, to stroke his ego. She had a complicated, crazy life and she didn't need the added stress of diving into a fling with a guy who, once they'd slept together, would quickly become bored of her and move on.

Kat leaned her butt against her car door and ran a hand over her face. She couldn't deal with this much sexy, not tonight, not now. Blinking at the burn in her eyes, she stared at her bare toes. "I'm not good company, Jonas. All I want to do is climb into my car and head on home."

"Tough day, huh?"

"Double shift, big bosses in the house, annoying guests, hotshot property developers who won't leave me alone," Kat said, trying for flippant but sounding sad instead.

"That bites. Headache?"

"A bitch of one," Kat replied, frowning when he pulled her away from the car so he could stand behind her. Kat whimpered when his strong thumbs and fingers dug into the taut muscles below her neck, beneath her shoulder blades. God, if he kept doing that she was going to dissolve into a puddle at his feet.

But, damn, it felt like heaven and she never wanted him to stop. Jonas moved his thumb up her neck to push it into the hollow at the base of her skull, and she whimpered as the sweet, sweet pain drained away her stress.

"You are crazy tense," Jonas whispered, his mouth directly above her ear. Kat shivered, this time from pure arousal. "Every muscle in your body is tight."

Kat managed to lift her shoulder. "It's been a rough few days."

Jonas dropped his arms over her chest, his forearms pressing into her breasts, creating a solid, warm X across her body.

Kat allowed him to take her weight, annoyed that he made her feel safe and secure and not so alone.

Jonas didn't speak, he just held her against him, his big body providing a place for her to rest. She wanted to burrow into him, to suck up some of his strength, both mental and physical. She wanted some of his confidence, his street smarts, his I-always-know-what-to-do attitude.

Because she didn't want to want him, she got pissy. "Isn't this where you ask me to come back to your room and promise you'll massage every inch of me until I feel boneless?" she asked, wincing at the bitchy note in her voice.

"I make an effort not to be predictable." Jonas's silk-over-steel voice rumbled in her ear.

Kat pushed her bottom into the hard length of him and wiggled against him. "That tells me different."

"You're a very sexy woman, Katrina, and that's what my body does when I'm holding a sexy woman. It doesn't mean I am going to jump you."

"Then what are you doing?" Kat asked, genuinely confused.

Jonas released his arms and gently turned her around. "Who, or what, have you been dating, Katrina? Neanderthals?"

Close. She'd married one.

"You looked like a woman who needed her neck rubbed, who could do with a hug," Jonas explained. "Someone who needed a friend."

"Oh," Kat said. She rubbed her forehead and squinted up at him. "So, you didn't come here to hit on me?"

Kat heard the note of disappointment in her voice and when Jonas laughed, she knew that he did, too. "Do you want me to?"

Kat shook her head and opened her mouth to issue a sharp retort, but Jonas's hand on her wrist made the words die on her lips. Without warning, he dipped his head and his mouth covered hers, his lips begging her to open up. She did and his tongue invaded her mouth, robbing her of coherent thought.

Kat could only grab his shirt, a T-shirt this time. She wrapped her hand in the fabric and held on. Jonas pushed his leg between her knees and pulled her closer, the full skirt of her dress allowing her to ride his hard, denim-covered thigh. Kat groaned and Jonas's hand moved up her leg, past her knee and under her dress to grip her thigh. His fingers were inches from the small triangle covering her.

God, she wanted him to touch her in the worst, best way.

This was insanity… They were in a parking lot and she was pulling herself across his leg, trying to get off, hoping he'd rocket her to an orgasm.

Jonas pulled his mouth off hers and rested his forehead against hers, his hot hand still gripping her thigh. "I promise that isn't why I'm here. Though I'm damned if I'll apologize for wanting you."

"I keep promising myself I won't kiss you again," Kat murmured. Promises aside, the reality was that she wanted more of those drugging kisses, the way he made her heart pound, her skin blister. She wanted him. But because she felt so out of control, she backed away.

Jonas swore, ran his hand across his lower jaw and swore again. He placed his hands on his hips and stared up at the black sky.

"Can I feed you? Buy you a drink? Coffee?" Jonas eventually asked, his voice back to normal.

"Sorry. It's late." And she was feeling fragile and unable to resist temptation.

"Tomorrow is Saturday. Are you working?" Jonas demanded, casually adjusting his tented pants before raking his hand through his hair.

"The lunch shift."

Jonas picked up her hand and slid his fingers between hers. "Tomorrow night, I'm going to feed you and we're going to have a chat."

Kat vehemently shook her head. "I'm not going to date you, Jonas." Was she trying to convince him or herself?

"Actually, I want to talk to you about a business proposition, something you might be interested in."

Kat frowned at his unexpected reply. "What kind of business proposal?" she asked, suspicious.

Jonas shook his head as he lifted his hand to brush his fingers across her cheek, into her hair. "You're tired and I can still see the headache in your eyes. We'll go into it tomorrow."

Kat, even more suspicious now, lifted her hands. "I'm not going to do anything illegal, Jonas."

Jonas pulled his fingers from hers and stepped back.

Despite the dim light of the parking lot she noticed his eyes had lightened, turned icy. Crap, her words had hurt him; she could see the sting in his eyes.

"Why would you think I would ask you to do something that wasn't aboveboard?" Jonas asked, moving out of her reach.

"I—" Kat started to lie then decided he deserved

the truth. She bit her bottom lip before forcing the words through slightly numb lips. “I read the financial publications, follow the business news. Your family isn’t known for playing by the rules.”

“I do,” Jonas snapped, his voice as harsh as a Siberian winter.

Kat saw him hunch his shoulders, dig his fists into the pockets of his jeans. She waited for him to speak again or to walk away, the chances were fifty-fifty.

“I’m my own man, Kat, so don’t judge me by what they do. Or did. See me for what I am. Judge me on my words and actions.”

Kat folded her arms and nodded her head.

“I need the words, Katrina.”

“I’ll judge you on what you say or do, not on your relatives’ reputations.”

Kat saw him expel a long breath, saw his tension dissipate. She lifted a shoulder. “So, are you still going to feed me tomorrow night?” she asked, wanting to know if she’d torpedoed their plans. She was curious to hear about his business proposal and, yeah, she wanted to see him again. She shouldn’t but she did.

Jonas nodded. “Yes, I am. Do you want me to come pick you up or do you want to meet me?”

“Uh…you don’t want to just chat at my place?”

“If I go to your place, not a hell of a lot of talking will happen. In our case, privacy would be distracting,” Jonas said, his tone dry. “Meet me at the Dolphin Fountain by Stearns Wharf at six thirty.”

Kat nodded. "Okay. Are you going to offer me a job?"

Jonas bent and dropped a kiss on her temple. "Tomorrow, Kat." Jonas placed his hand on the handle to her car door and frowned when it didn't open. He gave it another jerk and it popped free. "Kat, this car. It's…diabolical. Is it safe?"

"Safe enough."

"I'll follow you home."

Independence made her protest. "I'll be fine, Jonas."

"You have a splitting headache and have had a rough day. I'll follow you home to make sure you get there safely. Or you can leave your car here and I'll drive you. You can argue until dawn breaks, but those are your options."

Bossy man. Kat ducked under his arm and slid in behind the wheel. She jammed the key in her ignition, turned it and cursed when the engine spluttered and died. She cranked the engine again but nothing happened.

Kat muttered a small prayer, turned the engine again and smiled when the engine spluttered to life.

"It sounds like an asthmatic old man," Jonas said, his tone mournful.

"Do not diss my car. She's classic."

"She's scrap held together by rust, wheels and an engine," Jonas muttered, tapping the frame above her head. "I'll follow you home. Of course, I might be gray by the time we get there…if we get there at all."

* * *

The next night Kat approached the Dolphin Fountain from Carillo Street and scanned the people milling around the beachfront landmark. It was just after six thirty and Jonas was a little late. Kat, feeling nervous, sat on the edge of the cement ring and reminded herself that, in a little while, she'd have all the answers to the questions that had consumed her thoughts since she'd watched him drive away in his SUV.

Business proposition?

A deal?

Why was she so very attracted to him?

That last one was an easy question to answer, Kat thought, watching him walk toward her like he owned the town. He was sexy in his expensive suits and designer shirts, but dressed in cargo shorts, an olive green T-shirt and brown boat shoes, expensive, trendy glasses covering his eyes, he looked fantastic. Billionaire meets beach bum, Kat thought.

So hot.

Kat looked down at her outfit, glad she'd chosen to go casual. Her tangerine-colored, crocheted, off-the-shoulder top over a white camisole and battered, ripped denim shorts meant they would be avoiding the rarefied air of luxury establishments.

Jonas stopped in front of her and sent her a slow smile. "That's the first time I've seen your hair down." He looked down her back and whistled. "It really does hit your waist."

Feeling self-conscious, Kat gathered the strands in

her fist, rolled them into a long strand and dropped it again. "I keep meaning to get it cut but I need it to be a little longer before I do."

"You need it to be longer before you cut it? That doesn't make sense."

"If I cut it when it's another half inch they can make two wigs from the length instead of throwing a lot of the hair away."

Jonas frowned. "Wigs? Are you selling your hair?"

Kat smiled. "My financial situation isn't that dire, Halstead. I donate the hair to an organization that makes wigs for cancer patients, specifically children."

"Oh." His face softened and he looked ten years younger. "That's amazing. How did you hear about them?"

Through Cath first, but Kat wasn't ready to talk to him about her beloved, dying aunt. "I heard about the program and found a stylist who works with them. I grow my hair, Marcie cuts it off… It's a mutually beneficial arrangement."

Jonas pushed his sunglasses into his dark hair and stared at her, amusement and respect in his eyes.

Kat didn't like the warm feeling that rolled through her body.

"That's a nice thing to do, Kat. But I'm trying to imagine you with short hair."

"Short, edgy pixie cut." At his blank look, Kat smiled. "You don't know what a pixie cut is?"

"I understand 'pixie' and 'cut' but the two words together? No."

Kat stood and patted his arm. "I go from lots of hair to having not much." Kat couldn't believe they were discussing hairstyles when there were more interesting subjects to discuss. Case in point…

"So, want to tell me about this business deal?"

"I will." Jonas gestured that they should walk in the direction of Stearns Wharf. "Let's get a drink at one of the restaurants on the wharf and we can chat."

"Why not tell me now?" Kat demanded, impatient.

"It's complicated." Jonas looked down at her. "And I'd like to get a few drinks in you before I do."

It sounded like he was joking, but Kat suspected he wasn't. Oh, Lord, what was he going to ask her to do? Before she could demand more information, he changed the subject.

"Tell me something… That LCA exam you mentioned you were studying for? Is that part of the MBA program?"

Kat nodded. "Yeah."

"You're studying part-time?"

"I'm doing it one subject at a time, taking far too long for each. It's hard, I won't lie to you."

"Why didn't you finish it at college?" Jonas saw the expression on her face and grimaced. "Ran out of money, huh?"

"Yeah, between the divorce and my dad's death, staying in college wasn't an option."

Jonas placed a hand on her shoulder to stop her and Kat turned to look at him. "You were married?"

Kat nodded. "For a year or so."

"What happened?" Jonas asked, his voice gentle.

"I expected him to support me when my life fell apart, asked him to help me through a rough time. He chose not to."

"Asshat."

Wes really was, Kat silently admitted. "It was over four years ago and he taught me a couple of useful lessons."

"Like?" Jonas asked.

He might as well know, Kat thought. "Well, he taught me that the only person I can rely on is myself."

"That explains your rabid independence. What else?"

"Oh, just that I'll never get married again."

"Ah, crap," Jonas muttered, looking like he was gritting his teeth.

"And that would be a problem for you why?" Kat asked, her heart rate inching upward.

"Because I need you to marry me. And I need you to do it soon, like in the next two months."

Kat thought she'd heard Jonas suggest they get married. She shook her head and stared at him, not sure if he was joking.

He looked heart-attack serious but he had to be joking. Had. To. Be.

Kat, not knowing what to say to such an outrageous statement, allowed Jonas to take her hand and lead her into a restaurant on the edge of the water. In a daze, she followed him to an outside table, gratefully sinking into the chair Jonas pulled out for her. When he sat, he ran his hand through his hair and leaned back in his chair.

"Want a drink?" he asked.

"Hell, yes. I *need* a drink," Kat murmured and ordered a margarita. Icy, tangy and full of liquor, she was going to need one or three to navigate this conversation.

Jonas ordered a beer, and when the waitress skipped away, Kat drummed her fingers on the tabletop.

"Yep," Jonas said before she could speak. "I kind of, sort of, asked you to marry me."

"Was it a serious question?"

"Yes."

"Have you been drinking?" Kat demanded. "Are you high?"

Jonas shook his head. "I genuinely do need you to marry me, before the end of May."

"Why? Because you've fallen madly in love with me and you can't live another day without me?" Kat asked, her tone extra flippant.

"Would you believe that?"

"No. I don't believe in fairy tales," Kat stated, feeling calmer. She leaned forward and rested her forearms on the table between them. "Right, so why do you need to get married?"

Jonas looked at her, obviously debating how much to tell her.

"Jonas, I work at Harrison's flagship restaurant, it's filled with celebs every single night. I see husbands eating with their lovers. I see wives kissing the tennis pro. I see secret business meetings between sworn enemies. I could've sold those stories a hundred times over. I know how to keep my mouth shut."

Jonas nodded to the approaching waitress and waited until after she'd left before speaking again. "My grandfather is threatening to disinherit me unless I marry."

Kat couldn't believe what she was hearing. "That sounds positively medieval!"

"That's what I told him!" Jonas exclaimed.

"So…why?"

Jonas grimaced, looking uncomfortable. "When I was younger I dated a lot—"

"You still date a lot," Kat pointed out.

"Fair enough. But my grandfather was a lot more tolerant of my social life in my twenties than he is in my thirties. I should be married, according to him, preferably having sired male children to take over the business."

"God, I can't believe what I am hearing," Kat murmured.

"Believe it. My grandfather wants to ensure there will be more Halsteads after me and to do that I must marry. He's prepared to blackmail me to get me to take that first step."

"Is this legal? Can you challenge it?" Kat asked, taking a large sip of her margarita and sighing with pleasure as the lime and tequila slid down her throat.

"As it was pointed out to me, Jack can leave his stake in the company to anyone he likes and, if I don't dance to his tune, that person might not be me.

In fact, he told me it would *not* be me. I stand to lose the company I've devoted the past fifteen years to if I don't marry."

Kat rubbed the back of her neck, utterly out of her depth. "But why me, Jonas? I mean, there must be a bevy of beauties out there who would be happy to marry you."

"Maybe. But they want the real deal. They want the white wedding and an actual marriage and access to my bank accounts."

So cynical, Kat thought, but she supposed he had a right to be. With his wealth, he was a catch. Add sexy and, yeah, nice to the package and Kat could understand why many women would be happy to hitch themselves to his star.

Kat would prefer to ride her own star, thanks all the same. "Still, why me?"

"With you, I can make this a business deal. I know you need cash, and I know you need it quickly. I would be prepared to pay you. This…arrangement wouldn't last more than ten months, a year at the most. I would make that year of marriage to me worth your while."

She should shut this conversation down but she was—damn her curiosity—intrigued. "Worth my while how?" Kat asked, her heart in her throat.

"I'd pay you five hundred thousand for each month you were my wife, with the agreement that it will be a minimum of ten months, maximum a year."

Kat's fingers tightened around her glass and she had to remind herself to breathe. "That would cost you six million dollars," Kat whispered, gobsmacked.

"I'd expect you to sign a prenup. This would be a legal agreement."

Jonas had said it was a business deal, and he was discussing it that dispassionately. He needed a wife. He was prepared to pay for one. Kat needed money; he had it.

It would be the solution to so many of her problems.

"You could go back to college, finish your MBA. Get a job where you can use that brain of yours for more than allocating table seating."

Kat's mind raced. She could stay in her apartment. She could buy a new car, pay for that damn dress. She could help Cath find the care she needed. God, Kat would be free.

It was tempting.

It was insane.

"C'mon, Jonas, this is nuts. You can't be serious." Kat hoped he'd tell her he was joking. Then they'd laugh about the amazing prank he'd played on her.

Instead, Jonas just lounged in his chair, his finger tapping his beer bottle, looking far too calm for a man who'd just rocked her world.

Kat drained her margarita in one long gulp and banged the big-bowled glass onto the table. "Can you order me another?"

Jonas held up his near full bottle of beer. "You slammed that down. How about something soft before you pass out?"

Kat wanted to protest but knew he was right. Her head was already spinning from the combination of desire, tequila, six million dollars and a marriage proposal. Kat placed her elbow on the table, her chin in the palm of her hand. "So what would you expect from me?"

"Out of this marriage?"

Kat nodded.

Jonas looked away from her to a lithe blonde standing on a paddleboard just off the pier. But he wasn't actually seeing the woman, Kat realized. His thoughts were far away. "I don't know, I hadn't really planned that far ahead. I haven't thought beyond my showing my grandfather the wedding certificate and seeing his shares pass into my hands."

"Well, maybe you should think beyond that. Whether it's me or someone else, you'd have a woman in your life on a semi-permanent basis. Would you expect her to live with you? Where do you live, by the way?"

"I have an apartment in LA, not far from the Halstead headquarters. Currently, I'm renting a suite in a boutique hotel not far from here."

"Why are you here, in Santa Barbara? Don't you have people to oversee your projects? Aren't you needed in LA?"

"I work virtually and go back to headquarters for management and board meetings. I move from project to project. The Cliff House captured my imagination and I wanted to be around to watch the renovation."

"So where would your wife live?" Kat asked.

"Anywhere she wanted to. I'd rent a house or an apartment and pay for her living expenses, her car."

Kat gathered her courage and asked Jonas the question burning a hole in her stomach. "Sex?"

"What about it?"

Kat rolled her eyes. "Would it be part of the deal? Would you expect your fake wife to put out?"

"No… I don't know." When he saw her annoyance bubble up, his eyes flashed with anger. "All I mean by that is that I hadn't thought that far. Of course sex wouldn't be part of the deal. Will you please stop assuming the worst of me?"

God, even pissed he was sexy. His features became starker and his green eyes flashed. Man, she wanted him. So damned much.

And what did it say about her that she was feeling a tad disappointed that sex wasn't part of the deal?

"The marriage agreement would be totally separate from whatever happened in the bedroom." Jonas tapped the bottom of his beer bottle against the edge of the table, looking rattled. "I cannot believe I need to explain this!"

She'd hurt him, Kat realized. She hadn't meant to, but it had happened all the same. She had wanted to think badly of him. It was a defense mechanism. Pushing him away would keep her from feeling too much, from not just lusting over him but liking him. Lust she could handle; it was easy to dismiss. But liking him? Liking him was deeply problematic. Liking him led to love and love wasn't somewhere she was prepared to go. Not again.

"Sorry," Kat softly said.

Kat saw Jonas's hand tighten around his beer bottle and watched, fascinated, as he flexed his fingers. The tension and annoyance faded from his face after her apology. When his eyes met hers again, they were free of anger.

"I want you, you know that as well as I do. But sex is not part of the deal. If we end up in bed together, that would be a separate discussion. Clear?" Jonas asked, his tone even now.

"Clear," Kat responded.

Jonas waited awhile before picking up a menu and handing one to her. "What do you want to eat? Are you hungry?"

Marriage, sex, six million dollars and he was asking her what she wanted to eat? Kat had a quick mind but she was reeling. "You want to eat?"

"Sure, I'm starving."

Kat rubbed the space between her eyebrows with two fingers. "We were discussing marriage."

Jonas flipped his menu open and sent her a sympathetic look. "I've dropped a bombshell, Kat. I don't expect you to give me an answer today, or even tomorrow. Take some time to think about it."

He kept surprising her. She didn't like it that she didn't have him pegged. "I'll probably say no," Kat warned him. "I'm more of a bust-my-back than a take-the-easy-route type of girl."

"I know that." A small smile hit Jonas's lips. "Trust

me, you saying yes right away would be the biggest surprise of my life. But sometimes, very infrequently, miracles do happen."

Five

Of course she couldn't marry Jonas Halstead.

The idea was ridiculous, ludicrous.

Sure, marrying him would make her life easier. Money could do that. But accepting his offer would make her feel like a commodity, as if Halstead owned her the way he owned his expensive cars and his fancy suits.

She belonged to nobody; she never would. No, dammit, she'd do what she had to do on her own terms, by marching to the beat of her own drum.

Six million dollars. Six million reasons to say no.

Kat parked outside Cath's small house in San Roque, pulled her keys from the ignition and slid out from behind the wheel of her rust-bucket car. She squinted down at the wheels, thinking they were looking a little worn. The devil on her shoulder started to whisper, *One month being married to Halstead would do more than fix your tires*. It would change her life, flip it upside down, make it new and bright and shiny. One little ceremony, one signed contract and she'd be rescued.

Kat's stomach lurched and she swallowed once then twice. As Jonas's wife, she'd be able to forget the nights she'd spent wading through bills and trying to stretch one dollar into ten; the hours she'd spent making money to finish her postgrad degree; the arguments she'd had with her stepmom, begging June to release some funds so Kat could finish school.

Memories rolled in like an acidic, chemical tide. She'd screamed, cried and begged, but June had remained unmoved. Her father had left all his assets to his wife—cash, insurance policies and the contents of his house, including his first wife's personal possessions—and June had no intention of parting with any of it.

"Go ask your husband for cash," June had told Kat. "When you married, you became his responsibility." Wes, the tight-fisted bastard, had said no to money for school and not many weeks after that, he'd hurt Kat in the worst way possible.

Her father's sudden death, and his shocking will, had left Kat feeling unloved and unworthy. Sure, from day one she and June had fought, mostly because June deeply resented sharing her husband with his daughter. As a result, Kat's relationship with her dad had become strained. But Kat had never thought she would be cut out of his will. He could've, at the very least, left Kat her mother's photos, jewelry and mementos. The last time Kat had seen June she'd noticed her wearing Kat's mom's favorite pair of diamond studs. Kat had barely restrained herself from ripping the jewels from June's ears.

Kat wasn't sure if she could forgive her dad for that.

Jonas was also facing disinheritance, albeit on a larger scale. He stood to lose hundreds of millions, possibly billions, if he didn't marry, but Kat sensed he was less concerned about the money than he was about the company. Curious, she'd done some research on Halstead & Sons and there was no doubt that Jonas had, in recent years, turned the company around.

Pre-Jonas, Halstead had been rocked by scandals involving shoddy building practices, low wages, labor unrest and questionable business practices. Jonas had changed all that; business journalists frequently said he was as smart and tough as his predecessors but had a streak of integrity that seemed to be missing in the previous generations of Halsteads. Building practices had improved, safety practices were adhered to—and Halstead now paid some of the best wages in the industry.

Jack Halstead might own the shares but it was Jonas's company. She couldn't blame him for wanting to seal the deal.

But *marriage*?

Could she trust him to keep his word, to do what

he said? He'd spoken about prenuptial agreements, about legal contracts, but, as she well knew, documents could always be challenged. It was the actions that followed the words that mattered. Her father had said one thing—*I'll pay for your education, your mother's possessions will be given to you when the time is right*—and gone back on his word. Wes had promised to love, protect and care for her and he'd quickly forgotten those vows. He'd promised to be her husband, her best friend, her lover and her supporter. He'd turned out to be a bully with a low sex drive.

And she was considering marrying again? She couldn't, wouldn't…shouldn't. Offers like Jonas's were too good to be true. There had to be a catch somewhere. Yes, she would be a lot richer, but she knew that, with their combustible sexual attraction, they wouldn't be able to keep their hands off each other. They'd be sleeping together in no time. And if those lines between business and personal blurred, they'd end up with a complicated mess on their hands. Six million dollars wasn't worth the loss of her self-respect. Or her heart.

Besides, to marry him, she'd have to trust him, to a certain extent at least. She was still coughing up water because the two men she'd loved and adored had left her to drown.

And she was thinking about stepping into that murky lake again? She couldn't do it.

She used to be a trusting daddy's girl, a naive young wife. She was now smart and independent.

She'd clawed her way back to solid footing and she refused to depend on anyone. But she was also, she thought as she walked up to Cath's front door, still broke.

"Honey, I've been checking out hotties on that dating app!"

Kat, standing in the doorway of Cath's living room, dropped her bag to the floor and gave her aunt a once-over. Cath didn't look any worse than she had last week. That had to be a good sign.

They were waiting for the results of the latest blood tests, which would tell them if Cath would see her sixtieth birthday or not. So young, Kat thought, and so full of life.

"Find anyone you want to hook up with?" Kat asked after dropping a kiss on Cath's cheek. She sat on the edge of her aunt's armchair and looked down at Cath's tablet and into an admittedly handsome but far too young face. "Thirty-five years is too much of an age gap, darling. Even for cougars like you."

Cath's laugh was not as strong as it usually was. "Not for me, you twit, for you!"

Kat pulled away to frown at her aunt. "Are you trolling a dating app looking for a date for me?"

"Absolutely! I've had to hold myself back. I've only swiped right on twenty guys and most of them swiped back and fifteen of them want to meet you."

Whoa! What? Kat jumped up from her seat to glare at her aunt, slapping her hands on her hips.

"You registered me and now you are picking my

dates? What the hell, Cath?" Kat yanked the tablet from Cath's hand and saw the thumbnails of, yep, twenty guys on the screen. One was licking the handle of his mountain bike.

Kat spun the tablet around and pointed at the photos of men she'd never date. "These? What are you thinking? This one has his tongue frozen to a lamppost!"

"Oh, I think I must've swiped right when I was falling asleep once or twice."

"Or ten times!" Kat shook her head. "I am not meeting any of them!"

"Why not?"

Kat looked at the tablet again. "Too young. Too vain. Too in love with his motorbike. Psycho. Sociopath. Gym freak!"

"You're too picky," Cath grumbled.

Kat tossed the tablet onto the cushion of the sofa and blew out a frustrated breath. "Cath, I've got enough on my plate. I do not need to date weirdos."

"I'd be happy if you just dated someone, had some fun. Sex is an excellent way to relieve stress."

Kat opened her mouth to speak, realized she had nothing, and snapped it shut again. After a minute she shook her head. "Mom was such a lady. How is it possible that the two of you were twins?"

"Oh, I was swapped at birth. I'm actually the daughter of a billionaire."

If she never heard the word *billionaire* again it would be too soon.

Kat watched as Cath pulled in a deep breath, a

sure indication that a wave of pain was about to contract every muscle in her body. Cath panted slightly, closed her eyes, and Kat watched, helpless, as her aunt fought the pain. After a minute Cath finally relaxed, but she looked pale and defeated.

The pain medication wasn't strong enough, Kat realized as she knelt in front of Cath and placed her hands on her aunt's knee. "You're not getting better, are you?"

When she was first diagnosed with pancreatic cancer, Kat and Cath promised each other to always be honest. "No, I'm not." Cath picked up a strand of Kat's hair and wrapped it around her finger.

"And there is nothing else they can give you? Nothing else they can try?"

"This is the strongest medicine my insurance will pay for. After this, the next step is experimental drugs, clinical trials, being a human guinea pig."

Kat nodded. Right, then that's what they would do. Her mother's twin, her soul mother, would not succumb to this disease. Not without a fight and not until she'd tried every option available.

This was the woman who'd held Kat as she'd cried over her mom's coffin, whose house she'd run to when the walls of her own seemed to close in on her. Cath had taught her about the birds and the bees, taken her shopping, to the prom. Cath had taken the role of mother of the bride at Kat's wedding. Cath had dried Kat's tears, nursed her through her first hangover and breakup, held her hand through her father's death and through her divorce. Cath had stepped into her mom's shoes when June had refused to.

Cath was her home, the one place where Kat felt truly loved. Cath was the center of Kat's world and she couldn't lose her. She'd lost too much already…

"Right, then we'll do that. Who do I contact?"

Cath let out a small laugh. "My darling, Kat, so gung-ho. That's not going to happen, honey. Those trials are all taking place overseas, there's one happening in Switzerland, and it costs… God, the cost! Put it this way, between us we can't afford an air ticket let alone the cost of that treatment."

"I'll find the money," Kat stated, Jonas's face appearing behind her eyes.

"Kat, I'm not talking about ten thousand dollars, or even twenty. I'm talking big money. This is something I have to accept, darling girl, and so do you."

She didn't have to accept a damn thing. As long as they had options for Cath's recovery, or even just improvement, Kat wouldn't allow herself to imagine a world without Cath in it. As long as she had breath left in her body, she'd do everything in her power to keep Cath in her life.

She knew what she had to do.

She couldn't think about this, she just had to send the text message and get it done. If she wavered, if she hesitated, she would lose her courage and Cath would die. Maybe not today or tomorrow, or even in a year, but sooner than she should. Kat would not be able to live with herself if that happened. Especially if she could prevent it.

Hi, it's Kat.
Is that six-million-dollar offer still open? If it is, then I'm interested. Call me.

There, it was done. It seemed, she thought, tears burning in her eyes, she was getting married. For money.

Kat climbed to her feet and tucked her phone away. "Want some tea?" she asked.

"I'd prefer a double whiskey," Cath grumbled.

"Along with me meeting any of those men you swiped right for, that's not happening," Kat said, pulling her phone from her back pocket.

He'd replied already.

Kat,
I'm in Toronto. There's a problem on a project here that I need to resolve. The offer's still open but let's talk. I'll call you when I get back to town.

Decision made. Marrying Jonas would net her all the money she needed—but, oh, God, what would it cost her?

After her father died and she and Wes divorced, Kat made sure to always have a plan B…and a plan C. She never wanted to be caught off guard again. But if Jonas rescinded his offer, which was highly possible since she hadn't heard from him in four days, there would be little—nothing—she could do to help Cath. How would Kat live with that?

Kat slammed the door to her car shut and carried her bag and heels up the concrete path to her front door. She was exhausted. She'd taken every shift she could and that meant double shifts all week. Instead of sleeping, she'd spent all her free time on her computer, scouring the internet for information relating to the treatment of pancreatic cancer, hoping for a miracle treatment and praying that said miracle would be free.

Cath hadn't done enough research into the clinical trials in Switzerland and it turned out they had very strict criteria for who entered the program. Cath was too old, too sick, and her disease was too far along for them to consider her.

Kat stopped to pull a stone from the bottom of her flip-flop, thinking of thc information she'd found earlier. There was a California-based doctor who was also doing a similar treatment and, if Kat had access to cash, he might be an option. It all came down to money, as so much did.

"Kat, it's me. Don't scream."

A black shadow moved at the top of the stairs. Kat looked up and saw Jonas sitting on the step dressed in jeans and a plain black T-shirt. In the light from the corner of the landing she could see the stubble on his cheeks and jaw, his tired eyes.

"God, you have the survival instincts of a moth," Jonas grumbled. "You see a shadow, you run. At the very least you scream."

"I knew it was you," Kat said. She couldn't explain it, but she knew that if it had been anyone else but Jonas lurking around she would've screamed and run. It was like her subconscious, her soul, recognized him on a deeper level. How? And why him?

She was utterly exhausted but just seeing him gave her a bolt of energy; he was like a particularly potent elixir. And, as tired as she was, he still managed to stir her juices, to ratchet up her breathing and jump-start her heart.

He was such a man, Kat thought. Uncompromisingly masculine, hard-bodied and sharp-eyed. And she just wanted to crawl into bed with him and let him feed the hunger that raged inside of her.

Since that wasn't going to happen, she was happy just to stand here and stare at him, soaking him in.

"Get up here, Kat."

Kat walked up the stairs and sat next to him, dumping her bags and shoes behind her. She stretched out her legs and arched her feet, groaning at the pure relief.

"Long night?" Jonas asked, his shoulder against hers.

"Long couple of nights and days," Kat replied. "When did you get back?"

"This morning. I've been trying to call you all day but every time I picked up my phone I was slapped with another problem. By the time the calls stopped, it was after ten and I knew you'd be at work. So I went for a run, had something to eat and thought I'd wait for you here." Jonas nodded to the street where her car stood under a streetlight. "There's something seriously wrong with your car. I could hear it rattling long before you turned down the street."

Kat pulled a face. "I'm just grateful it's still running."

"Two words. *Scrap yard.*"

"Another two words. *No money,*" Kat replied. "Are you happy to sit here? It's such a nice night and my neighbor is away for two weeks, so talking out here won't disturb anyone."

Jonas leaned back and placed his elbows on the step behind him. "Okay."

Kat wiggled her toes and wondered how to address the big, sparkly elephant sitting on the steps with them. She was about to ask him if he'd changed his mind when Jonas spoke. "I was incredibly surprised to get your text message. I thought it would take a lot more persuasion to get to yes."

"I had every intention of saying no, I really did," Kat admitted, playing with the hem of her cobalt blue shift dress.

"Then why did you change your mind? What happened?"

Could she tell him? Could she open up a little and share why she was now prepared to forgo her independence and do this deal? Did she have a choice?

"I'm an only child and my mother died when I was fourteen. My dad remarried six months after her death and June, my stepmom, is…difficult. Before my mom's death, my dad and I were best friends, but June didn't like how close we were and she drove us apart. I ended up spending most of my time with my aunt Cath, who is my mom's twin."

"Is your dad still alive?"

"He died five years ago. He had a heart attack." Kat's voice dropped and she felt that familiar anguish and grief close her throat, burn her nose.

Jonas placed his hand on the back of her neck and immediately she relaxed. How did he do that?

"He left everything he had, every cent, to June. He did leave me my childhood home, but June has the right to live in it until she dies and I have to pay for its upkeep."

"Ouch," Jonas said, keeping his hand on the back of her neck. She was grateful. She felt anchored, centered. "Your stepmom won't help you out?"

Kat let out a low, bitter laugh. "If I were on fire, June would add some gas."

Not wanting to get bogged down in that swamp of past hurts, Kat quickly moved on. "Cath, on the other hand, is a gem. She paid for my last semester at college so I could get my degree."

"She sounds like a winner," Jonas said softly.

"She is. She's been my rock, my best friend, my second mom."

Jonas's thumb rubbed the cord in her neck. "But?"

She could tell him this; she could explain. He'd understand. "Around the time she paid for me to complete my undergrad degree, she was diagnosed with a rare form of pancreatic cancer. And it's hit her hard. She's a vibrant, funny, crazy, free spirit, but now she's chair- and bed-bound and it's killing me." Kat released a sad laugh at her accidental choice of words. "I mean it's killing *her.* Anyway, there's nothing more the doctors can do for her here in Santa Barbara. My lack of cash and their lack of experience dealing with this form of cancer are both stumbling blocks.

"But there's a doctor, working out of a private clinic in Malibu called Whispering Oaks. He's a researcher and he's looking for test subjects who would be willing to give something ridiculously unorthodox a try. He's had some fantastic results using a combination of homeopathic remedies and hard drugs."

Kat stared down at the street, her shoulders slumped. "It sounds like the answer to our prayers. It's expensive, but if you…um, paid me to marry you, I could swing the cost."

"And pay for the dress."

Kat didn't smile at his attempt at humor. "Money is the first problem, but there are others."

"Like?"

"The waiting list is a thousand deep and filled with younger people, people with families, teenagers, children. Intellectually, I understand the doctor choosing those younger patients, but this is Cath. I want them to choose her! She might be an unlikely candidate on paper but she's everything to me!"

Jonas pulled her to him, his arm around her shoulders. "Shh, honey. It's okay."

Kat found herself turning to him, burying her head in his neck, unable to stop the tears she'd been holding back for months, years. She shouldn't be crying. She couldn't afford to show him she was weak, needy. But the more she tried to stem her tears, the harder she tried to stop her sobs, the more they demanded to be released.

We've been strong for too long, her soul and her heart whispered. *Let us weep. We'll be strong again later. We'll pull ourselves together, pick up our broken pieces, but for now, just let us cry.*

So Kat did. She retreated from Jonas, wrapped her arms around her knees and silently sobbed. Tears wet her knees and ran down her legs, dropped onto the mosaic-tiled steps below. And Jonas allowed her to weep, his broad hand drawing circles on her back, giving her an anchor when grief threatened to wash her away.

Eventually her tears lessened and her sobs quieted. He held out the hem of his T-shirt, lifting the fabric to run the soft cotton over her cheeks, down her chin. He held the fabric in front of her nose. "Want to blow?" he asked.

Kat reared back, shocked. "I am *not* going to blow my nose on your T-shirt!"

"Thank God." Jonas smiled, dropping his shirt. He cocked his head. "Better?"

"Yes, thanks." The heat of embarrassment dried the tears Jonas had missed.

"I'm sorry about that." Kat pushed her hair back, lifted her shoulders. "I'm just so tired, so utterly wrung out. It's difficult being strong, day after day, night after night. I'm so tired of the responsibility. I keep waiting for the next wave of trouble to hit me, wondering if this one will finally drown me."

A sob, one of the few she'd suppressed, escaped.

"Shh, Kat." Jonas's hand drifted over her head as he pulled her closer. "Stop crying now, you're going to make yourself sick."

"Can't afford to get sick," Kat muttered into his neck, her arms wrapped around him. He smelled so good, like sunshine and comfort and heat. If she could stay there until she felt better, stronger, she'd be so grateful.

Jonas slid an arm under her legs and, without any effort, stood while holding her cradled against his body. "Where's your key, Kat?"

Kat opened her hand to show him the key she'd been holding since she'd left her car. Jonas nodded and walked to the entry. He balanced her across his lifted knee and managed to unlock the front door. Without turning on any lights, he walked through her apartment and into her bedroom, and gently placed her on her bed. He looked down at her as he pulled her flip-flops off her feet.

"You need to sleep, Kat." Jonas gently lifted her dress, pulling it up and over her hips and chest. Kat, too tired for embarrassment and feeling utterly safe, lifted her arms. After Jonas tossed the dress onto a chair, he put a big hand on her shoulder and pushed her down. Kat snuggled her head into her soft pillow and felt her eyes closing. Forcing them open, she tried to make eye contact with Jonas. "We need to talk. About getting married. About your offer."

"We will, but not now," Jonas told her, reaching for a cotton throw at the bottom of the bed and draping it across her legs and hips. "Sleep now, Kat. We'll sort it out later. There's time."

Kat, feeling safe and secure for the first time in years, closed her eyes and drifted off to sleep.

Six

Shortly after lunch the next day, Jonas stepped into the expensive lobby of El Acantilado and looked into the restaurant, wondering if there was ever a time the place wasn't hopping. He stood off to the side, watching Kat walk swiftly back to her station, her nice-to-see-you smile on her lips.

That smile didn't reach her eyes, Jonas realized, pushing the lapels of his black jacket aside so he could put his hands into the front pockets of his stone-colored chinos. She'd slept but it didn't look as if it had been a restful sleep. Her eyes were red-rimmed and makeup didn't quite hide the twin stripes of pale purple beneath her lower lashes.

The guests coming to eat at the famous West Coast restaurant wouldn't give their hostess a second thought. But to him, Kat was worth more than one thought, or even ten. Unfortunately she was pretty much all he thought about from the moment he opened his eyes.

And not just in the "I need to marry her soon, let's get this done" way. He'd had many thoughts of her naked, of course. He was a male who liked sex, a *lot* of sex. But in between those hot fantasies of kissing her from tip to toe and everywhere in between, he remembered her laugh, her silky hair between the tips of his fingers, the sadness and vulnerability in her eyes. He wanted to hold her, protect her, make her life easier, dammit.

What had happened to viewing his marriage as a business deal? When did this become so very complicated? Since meeting her, Kat Morrison had made steady inroads into his mind and, somehow, crept under the wall surrounding his heart, and she was lodged in there, walking all over his soul. This wasn't good, Jonas decided right then, and it certainly was not to be tolerated.

He was marrying Kat only because Jack said Jonas had to marry *someone*. This arrangement wasn't about happiness or death-do-us-part. This was a hard, simple business deal. That was all it ever could be.

He didn't do emotions and he didn't do entanglements. He certainly had no intention of doing either with his bride-for-hire.

Maybe it would be easier to marry Gigi or one of the other many women who'd crossed his path recently. None of them had ever caused his stomach to flip or his heart to stutter. Around them he could easily keep his emotional distance.

No.

No way would he marry one of those vapid women. Jonas shuddered. He'd prefer Jack shoot him.

Kat caught Jonas's eye, flushed, looked at the crowd of people waiting for her attention and held up a finger, asking him to wait. He nodded and he couldn't help a small smile at her embarrassment, knowing she was more ashamed of her tears than she was of him seeing her in her underwear.

Plain white. No frills. Sexy as hell. Walking away from that smooth skin and those long legs and that slim but curvy body had taken an enormous amount of effort.

He wanted her.

He was going to marry her.

He was going to have to keep his hands off her.

Jonas pushed his shoulder into a steel-clad wall and stared down at the floor, his thoughts in turmoil. They had to keep sex out of the equation, as difficult as it would be. The more he came to know her, the more she intrigued him. Fantastic sex would amplify those emotions. He couldn't afford to think of her as anything other than a business partner, a means to an end.

She needed cash from him, and she needed his connections. He needed a wife in name only because, as he'd checked and double-checked, Jack had never once mentioned that love had to be part of the deal.

Love would *not* be part of the deal. He didn't want it and he didn't need it. It was a cunning and dangerous emotion.

He wanted no part of it.

He could deal with no sex. He wasn't a kid anymore. Lack of sex wouldn't kill him…

But trying to keep his hands off Katrina might.

"Hi. Sorry to keep you waiting but it's been crazy busy."

Jonas straightened and looked over at Kat, standing behind her modern, free-form desk, her eyes reflecting fear and confusion. They needed to talk, to nail down this arrangement. Jonas looked around and saw that the lobby was empty. "Can you take a break?"

Kat looked at her watch and nodded. "I've already asked my manager to watch my desk and answer my phone."

Jonas walked out of the restaurant. Once in the sunshine outside, he shrugged out of his jacket. He looked down to the beach below, enjoying the sun on his face as he waited for Kat to join him. When she did, she gestured for him to turn right. "Let's walk in the vegetable garden around the back. I often take my breaks on the benches under the trees."

They walked to the back of the restaurant and into an area he hadn't known existed. The garden consisted of raised beds edged by zinc sheets, glinting in the sun. He saw fat, purple eggplants and bright red cherry tomatoes, and he inhaled the scent of lavender as Kat pulled her hand through the leaves of the herb as she passed it. Under the cypress tree, as she promised, was a bench. Kat sat on the edge, her hands tangled together.

"I'm sorry I lost it last night. I never cry and I don't know why I did."

Jonas noticed her flushed chest, the red tide creeping up her neck. It was a sure sign, he was coming to realize, that she was upset or embarrassed.

"Don't worry about it." Jonas sat next to her and stretched his arms out along the back of the bench, tipping his head to look up into the branches of the cypress. "This is a pretty spot."

"Yeah, it is," Kat said, running the palms of her hands on her pencil skirt. "Jonas—"

He wasn't sure what she was about to say but he wasn't going to give her a chance to back out from their deal, to have second thoughts. "Your aunt has an appointment at Whispering Oaks in a month's time. It was the earliest time they could fit her in."

Kat looked shocked, hopeful and confused all at the same time.

"But… *What?* There's a long waiting list!"

Right, time to explain how life worked in his world. "I know people, Kat, I know influential people. One of the benefits of money, and having the Halstead surname, is the ability to get what you want when you want it. I called someone and he called someone and an appointment was created."

"But who has that sort of clout?" Kat demanded, looking absolutely flummoxed.

This was going to be interesting. "Your boss."

"Jose? The restaurant manager?" Kat sounded skeptical.

"No, sweetheart. Harrison Marshall."

Confusion turned her dark blue eyes smoky. "I don't understand any of this."

He could see that. Jonas sat up, leaned forward and rested his forearms on his knees, allowing his hands to dangle between his legs. "In certain circles, Harrison has a reputation for being a guy someone can call when they want something done. Harrison collects contacts and connections like hoarders collect trash. He also likes doing favors for people."

"But Harrison is your direct competitor, why would you call him of all people?"

"He's a competitor in business—we sometimes bid for the same projects—but he's more than that. He's known me since I was a kid, so I felt comfortable asking him for a favor."

And, hopefully, Jonas thought, he wouldn't ask for ten pounds of flesh when he called in his IOU.

"But how and why would Harrison have the clout to get Cath an appointment?" Kat cried, trying to make sense of the bombshell he'd dropped in her lap.

"Does it matter?" Jonas asked. Harrison and his wealth of contacts was a conundrum and Jonas's gut instinct demanded he not look too closely at his old friend's actions. He wasn't sure he wanted to know…

Kat frowned at him. "Does Harrison know about Cath?"

Hell, no. Harrison was a friend but he wasn't that good a friend. Nobody was. "He doesn't. After I assured him that this favor wasn't for Jack, myself or anyone he knew, I asked him to get the appointment. I didn't tell him who it was for."

"Harrison knowing Cath was related to me would complicate the matter, so thank you. He recently gave me a raise by refusing to let me pay any rent on my apartment, so I'd feel uncomfortable if he knew he was helping me out again."

"This situation is plenty complicated enough," Jonas agreed. "Your aunt has an appointment with someone who should be able to help her, Dr. Cranston. He requires a deposit. He wants her to book into the clinic for a battery of tests and to monitor her condition. It will be very expensive."

"And the only way I can pay for it is if I marry you," Kat said, her voice bleak.

"Pretty much." Jonas felt frustrated at her despondent tone. "Kat, look, I'm not any happier about this than you are! I don't want to get married, but the situation is clear. I need a wife, you need money. It's a business deal—" maybe if he said it often enough, he would start to believe his own words "—so...are you in or are you out?"

He still thought there was a chance she'd say no, so he held his breath, waiting for the ax to fall. He was surprised when she nodded her head. "Yes, Jonas. We have a deal."

Well, hell. He'd just officially acquired a fiancée. His company was almost in his hands...

"Okay, good. Great," Jonas stated, his voice harsher

than he'd intended. Why did he feel bleak, like something was missing?

God, catch a clue, dude! Concentrate on what matters…

He needed a marriage certificate, the transfer of shares into his hands. He couldn't risk Jack changing his mind again. He needed to tell Jack, to tell the world, that he was marrying. Once the story was in the public domain, it would be a lot harder for Jack, or Kat, to back out. "Today is Thursday, what about Saturday?"

Kat blinked, gasped and blinked again. "To get married? Are you insane?"

Probably. "Not to get married, to host an engagement party. We can host it at the Polo Club."

Kat shook her head as if to clear it. She held up her hand, her gesture telling him that he was getting carried away. "It's the Polo Club, Jonas. It's booked up for months, years in advance for weddings. And we don't need a fancy engagement party."

Yeah, he kind of did. "It's expected, Kat. And I spoke to Mariella Marshall, who, as you know, runs the event planning arm of Harrison's company. She can do a party for a hundred people in the smaller of the two ballrooms any Saturday this month. But only if I give her a free hand with regard to the flowers and the food."

"But how did you explain the haste, the lack of a firm date?"

Jonas grinned. "I told her the truth. I told her that I was working on getting a girl to marry me and that

I needed to move fast once she said yes. She said that no girl she knew would consent to a hasty engagement party or wedding and I told her mine would. And then I told her that if she didn't think she could arrange the party or the wedding on such short notice, I'd bring someone down from LA."

"And she took offense at that and told you she absolutely could handle a last-minute event. You played her," Kat stated.

Jonas wasn't sure if her expression was a reflection of her horror or her admiration.

Yeah, he'd had the balls to manipulate Mariella Marshall. God, after maneuvering his father out of the business, dealing with Mariella Santiago-Marshall was a walk in the park.

Jonas shrugged. It was what it was. "So, do we have a deal?"

Kat was scared, he could see that. But she was going to say yes because she was prepared to do whatever she could for someone she loved, someone who obviously loved her. Lucky Kat, to love and be loved like that. He wondered what that felt like.

Being loved by Kat, who was loyal, honest and courageous—someone who had so much integrity—would be a hell of thing. Not that he knew how to handle unconditional love. He was more familiar with approval that had strings attached. In his family, that wishy-washy emotion ebbed and flowed with his performance. He wasn't perfect and he frequently did things his way, so Jack's approval was often withheld and love was never part of the equation.

Jonas had learned to live with it, but sometimes, when he was faced with someone else's example of real love, he wished he knew what it felt like.

But if wishes were horses and all that crap…

It was what it was. He couldn't change Jack. Jonas had no interest in his father's attention and his mother was, at best, crazy.

He'd drawn the short straw with regard to his family. Having to organize a hasty engagement party with a woman marrying him for money wasn't, sadly, even a surprise. It was just another example of his dysfunctional family life.

Lots of money? Lots of problems.

"We have a deal," Kat told him, and Jonas noticed the tremble in her voice, her shaking fingers, "on one condition."

He braced himself and mentally tried to work out what her angle could be.

"I need the world to think that we met and fell in love, that we can't wait to get married. I am going to lie my ass off to Cath. She's an absolute romantic and needs to hear that I am happy and settled and in love. I am also going to tell her you used your connections to get her into the trial for free… I don't want her worrying about who is paying for her treatment. I expect you to back me up in that lie."

That was her additional demand? Easy enough.

But there was more, he could see it in her eyes.

"And I will only take the money I need for her treatment, down to the last dollar. If you pay Whispering Oaks, I will stay married to you for a minimum of ten months and a maximum of a year."

Jonas heard the determination in her voice and scratched his head. She wanted less money, not more?

It was honorable but it wasn't going to work. "Kat, you need to look like my wife, act like my wife. And that means me spending money on you. Dresses, car, apartment. You're going to have to give up your job."

Kat sent him a look full of steady regard. "Oh, hell, no, I'm not giving up my job. When you walk out of my life, I need an income to pay the bills."

"Finish your damn degree and get a proper job in a field that excites you."

Kat shook her head. "Not on your dime."

"You're being ridiculously, stupidly independent."

"You can pay for the dress you ruined, if that makes you feel better."

It didn't. "Kat—"

Kat looked at her watch and rose. "I need to get back to work. I've taken more time than I should have."

"What will everyone think when my wife carries on working as a hostess?" Jonas demanded, following her to her feet.

Kat shrugged. "Then you should not have chosen me as a wife, Jonas. I need your money for Cath. That's all I'm prepared to take. I can't take more."

Jonas shook his head, frustrated. Of all the women in California, the one he wanted to marry had no interest in having access to his limitless credit card? "Then we don't have a deal."

Kat spun on her heel, her eyes shooting blue fire. "Excuse me?"

Whoa…*hot*. He'd seen tired Kat and professional Kat, even sexy Kat, but the fire in her eyes sent a bolt of arousal straight down his spine and into his junk. He was, suddenly and ridiculously, turned on. What he wouldn't do to slide his hand up and under that dress, to feel that creamy skin under his fingers, to taste her spicy mouth.

Business deal, Halstead, he reminded himself. *Bus-i-ness.*

Jonas worked hard to pull his attention back to their argument. "I pay for your clothes, your expenses, whatever you need for the next year. Take it or leave it."

"Are you really going there, Jonas? You need *me*," Kat said, folding her arms across her torso.

Jonas gave a little shrug. "I need a woman to marry me, Kat. Any woman. I like you, but you're not the only fish in the pond. How many rich men do you know who are prepared to pay you to marry them?"

Kat narrowed her eyes and tapped her foot. "You're bluffing."

He was and was surprised she'd picked up on it. "That's the deal, Kat."

"Asshat," Kat muttered, annoyed. She lifted a finger and Jonas knew he had her. "I want a contract. I want detailed expense reports kept. No expensive jewelry, ridiculously priced dresses and shoes. Buy me a car and I will disembowel you."

Jonas just held her hot stare. "A contract, yes. I'll agree to keeping the jewelry simple. Designer clothes are a necessity—"

"Then you have to buy them from my friend Tess at The Hanger so she can earn the commission," Kat argued.

He nodded. He was, reluctantly, touched by her generosity to her friend. "The car goes." Jonas held up his own finger. "Not. Negotiable. It's a death trap."

"Something small, inexpensive, and you'd better run the make and model past me before you buy it. It gets sold when we divorce," Kat countered, her color up and her eyes flashing. She was enjoying the negotiating, Jonas realized with a smile. Her blood was up and she wanted to win.

"Anything else?" Jonas asked, entertained.

"I'm sure there is," Kat retorted, her brow furrowed in concentration.

"We'll add all we've discussed to the prenup."

Kat raised her eyebrows. "So you don't trust me?"

She didn't need to sound so damn happy about it. He did actually trust her, and that scared the hell out of him. He didn't usually trust anyone. "It's standard procedure."

Kat released a panicky laugh. "Oh, Jonas, nothing about this is standard procedure!"

Jonas lifted his hands to hold her face, her skin soft under his rough fingers. "It'll be okay, Kat."

He dropped his head to kiss her temple, not trusting himself anywhere near her mouth.

"I hope so." Kat pulled her head back and held his wrist, her eyes locking on his. "Is having complete control of the company worth this, Jonas? Is being in control worth all this drama?"

Jonas took a long time to answer her. "No, maybe not." He saw the flash of disappointment in her eyes, tinged with sadness. "But making sure that someone else doesn't take control is worth every penny."

He'd said too much. Jonas dropped his hands and stepped back. "I'll let you get back to work and I'll do the same. I keep forgetting that I have a hotel to renovate, a massive company to run. We'll speak later, okay?"

Kat nodded and turned away, her hips swaying as she walked up the steps to the restaurant. When she reached the top, Jonas spoke again. "Kat?"

Kat turned around, lifting her hand to shield her eyes from the glare. "Yes?"

"Thanks." It was inadequate but he meant what he said. He was grateful. Profoundly.

"Ditto, Jonas. I wouldn't be doing this unless it was important. Cath means the world to me."

He knew she was trying to justify her actions, hoping he wouldn't think less of her because she was prepared to marry a stranger for money. Strangely, he wanted her to understand that his mission was just as important, that this wasn't all about shares and stocks and his inheritance. "I have other reasons, too, Kat. And they are equally valid."

Kat looked like she was going to demand what they were and he wondered whether he could trust her enough to tell her, shocked that he wanted to. How could he tell her that until he freed himself from Jack, from his father, from their lack of integrity, that he couldn't feel like his own man? Would she understand or would she think him weak for pandering to Jack's wishes for so long?

Jonas was confused by the sudden urge to open up, to reassure this woman that he wasn't the cold, hard-hearted businessman the world perceived him to be. He actually wanted to let her peek through a crack in the wall.

Jonas shook his head, feeling discombobulated and off center. Time to go…

"I'll call you," Jonas told her, turning away.

He would. But only much, much later—when he got his rebel heart back on its leash.

Jonas waited impatiently for Kat at the bottom of the main stairs of the Polo Club. Pushing back the cuff of his tuxedo jacket, he glanced at his watch and decided that if he didn't see her on the stairs in two minutes he'd barge into the penthouse and drag her out by her heels.

Jonas, his hand in the pocket of his pants, fiddled with the engagement ring he'd spent far too much time choosing. If it had been any other woman, he would've bought the biggest, boldest, most expensive ring in the store and be done with it.

Judging by her arguments about money—her new

car was still a point of contention between them; she'd also objected to dressing at the Polo Club, saying that hiring a room for her at the venue was a waste of money—he knew she wouldn't appreciate a big, flashy ring.

But she did deserve something unusual, exotic, classy, and he'd eventually settled on a fire-orange opal and diamond ring. God help him if she didn't like it; he wasn't going to spend another afternoon looking at tray after tray of rings.

Once was enough.

Right, he was going after her. Jonas put his foot on the first stair when he heard movement above him, and he slowly raised his eyes. God, she looked…

Stunning. Amazing. Fantastic…

None of the adjectives adequately conveyed the sensation rumbling around his chest. She was dressed in a structured white crop top and full ball-gown skirt the exact orange of the fire opal in his pocket. She'd pulled all that glorious hair back from her face and up into a style that reminded him of those animated princesses in Disney movies. Earrings dangled from her ears and she'd kept her makeup natural.

She looked… God, she looked sensational. And nervous. She rested her hand on the banister, closed her eyes and Jonas saw her lips move, as if in a silent prayer.

"Kat."

Kat's eyes flew open and Jonas saw worry flash in her gaze, uncertainty. She stared down at him, her fear tangible.

“What the hell are we doing, Jonas?” she softly asked and her words floated down to him.

“It’ll be okay, Kat. I promise.” Jonas’s own hand gripped the banister as if it were a life buoy in a turbulent sea. If he let go, he’d race up the stairs, march her down the corridor and take her straight to bed. That was how much he wanted her, how desperately he wanted to slip off that tiny top, how much he wanted to see that skirt in a froth of fabric on the floor. He wanted her naked and panting and he wanted her now.

“Are you okay?” she asked, concerned.

Jonas managcd a small smilc. “Just trying to gct my heart to restart. You look spectacular. Dazzling.”

Kat’s mouth tipped up at the corners as she started to walk down the stairs. “Thank you. You look pretty good, too.”

He was wearing a tuxedo, a white shirt, a black tie. Nothing special, but he appreciated the comment. Jonas waited for her to reach him and when she did he leaned forward to kiss her cheek, needing to make a connection with her, however small. Her scent was delicious and Jonas felt his head swim. What was wrong with him? He’d dated and slept with some of the most beautiful women in the world, but none of them had ever made him feel this off balance.

“You’re very late, Katrina,” he murmured, trying to get a handle on the situation.

Kat winced. “Lunch service ran over, my car wouldn’t start, traffic was hell.”

"Give up work, choose a damn car and I offered to send a driver for you."

Kat smiled and his heart stopped. Before the end of this evening Jonas suspected he might need a defibrillator. Kat smoothed her hand down his tie, over his chest. "I am not going to argue with you, Halstead. Not tonight."

Jonas smiled and lifted her knuckles to his lips. "Thank God for small mercies." Dropping his hand, he hooked his index finger in the band on her skirt, wishing he could lick the strip of bare skin between the skirt and her short top. "I'm glad you wore this and not the black-and-white dress."

Kat narrowed her eyes. "There's nothing wrong with that dress but Tess told me she left it behind and, because I was late, I had to choose between the three dresses she brought from the boutique."

Kat didn't need to know that he'd told Tess to make sure she left the dress behind. He smiled. "So, did you like the other two dresses?"

"I did," Kat reluctantly admitted. "The gold dress is fantastic."

"Good. The tags have been removed from all three so don't even think about returning them. You now have dresses for the next two formal functions we attend, so we won't have to have the don't-bother-buying-a-dress argument for another two weeks or so."

"You are diabolical," Kat told him, unhooking his finger from her skirt and squeezing his hand.

Jonas twisted his fingers so they linked with hers.

"Nope, I just like getting my way. And not arguing about money."

"Spoiled rich boy," Kat muttered, but he saw the smile in her eyes.

"Ridiculously independent, financially challenged girl," Jonas responded.

"Financially challenged?" Kat asked, her words coated with laughter. "You can just say poor. I'm not easily offended."

Jonas felt his heart stutter, told it to calm the hell down. He couldn't stop himself from kissing her mouth, one gentle touch of his lips against hers, a light flicker of his tongue. It was all he would allow himself or that dress was coming off, here at the bottom of the stairs.

Since that would be desperately embarrassing, Jonas eased back and wondered who this sap was who seemed to have taken over his body. God, he was acting like a kid, not like a grown man who had a deal with this vision—with this *woman*, he hastily corrected himself.

An outrageously sexy woman, but that shouldn't have any bearing on the subject. They were going to wed in a marriage agreement that was advantageous for both of them. *Keep your eye on the end goal, Halstead.*

That reminded him. He shoved his hand into the pocket of his pants, keeping his eyes locked on Kat's exquisite face. "I have something for you."

Jonas held the ring between his thumb and forefinger and watched as pleasure danced across Kat's face. “It’s a fire opal, set with diamonds, and it’s not expensive, so don’t start on at me about the cost.”

Kat didn’t say anything. She just took the ring and examined it from every angle, seemingly fascinated by the irregular shape of the stone.

“It’s unusual, I grant you that, but I thought you might like it,” Jonas said, uncomfortable with her silence. Damn, he’d really thought she would like it. “I can take it back if it doesn’t suit you. We’ll just tell anyone who asks that your engagement ring is being designed—”

Kat lifted up on her toes and dropped a quick, hard, openmouthed kiss on his lips. It shocked him. “Shut up, Halstead. I absolutely love it! It’s perfect.”

“It is?”

Kat slid the ring onto the appropriate finger and held her hand up to look at it. “It’s amazing, exactly what I would’ve chosen! Did you pick it to match my dress?”

Thanking God that she’d finally asked him a question he could answer without stuttering, Jonas smiled. “That was a happy coincidence.”

“Thank you for listening to me,” Kat said, her voice dropping in volume and increasing in intensity. “Thank you for not buying a whopping diamond or an expensive stone that I would’ve felt uncomfortable wearing.”

“It was my pleasure,” Jonas replied, not knowing what else to say. How did one respond when a gorgeous woman thanked you for not spending too much money on her?

It was one of the many mysteries he would have to unravel now that Kat Morrison had walked into, and upended, his life.

Seven

It was exhausting being the center of attention, Kat thought, edging behind a huge palm tree in the corner of the room. She just needed a moment or two alone, to catch her breath, to understand that this was now her life. Through the thick palm fronds, Kat looked across the ballroom to where Jonas was talking to a group of men. One of them was Rowan Brady, who'd shared Jonas's table that fateful night three or so weeks ago. Three weeks? Was that all the time that had passed? Sian was also here, flaunting her tattoos, much to the endless fascination of the guests and the disapproval of Jonas's grandfather.

Jack Halstead looked exactly how Kat imagined Jonas would when he reached old age. A thick head of hair, a craggy face dominated by fiercely intelligent eyes. When she was introduced to him earlier, Jack had acted like an absolute gentleman, nothing in his manner suggesting that he'd blackmailed his grandson into marriage. Actually, she rather liked the old man. He was charming and genial, but she knew he wasn't someone to be messed with.

In contrast, Kat did not like Lane, Jonas's father. At all. He'd kissed the back of her hand with fleshy lips that made her skin crawl. Kat felt like he had X-ray eyes that were mentally stripping her. It also interested Kat that Jonas seemed to dislike his father as much as she did. Jonas treated Jack with respect but his body tensed when he had to interact with Lane. He sounded genial but Kat could sense the angry currents swirling beneath their polite conversation. Kat wondered if anyone else knew that father and son loathed each other. Jack certainly seemed to be oblivious to the tension.

Not your business, Kat told herself. *You're in this dress and wearing this stunning ring for the bucks, remember? Do not get sidetracked by your curiosity about your sexy fiancé.* Kat darted another look at Jonas and sighed. It should be illegal for a man to look so good in a basic, albeit shockingly well-tailored, tux.

Dragging her eyes off Jonas, Kat realized that Jack and her boss were on the other side of the palm, both oblivious to her presence. Kat stood statue-still, hoping neither would notice her.

"Jack," Harrison said, tapping his crystal glass filled with expensive whiskey against Jack's beer glass. Kat rather liked the fact that Jonas's grandfather drank beer at a black-tie event. Maybe the Halsteads weren't as stuffy and snobby as she'd expected them to be. "I'm glad to see that you managed the Jonas situation without my help."

"Your help is expensive," Jack said, his tone amused.

"That it is. But young Jonas has made a good choice," Harrison said. "Katrina is the real deal."

"This is only the engagement. Nothing changes until I see them say I do," Jack replied and Kat heard the steel in his voice.

"Are you sure this is the only option?" Harrison asked.

"It's the only way I can protect the company. Jonas is the only person I trust implicitly."

That was a hell of a thing to say, Kat thought. She wondered if Jonas knew how highly his grandfather valued him.

"Well, call me if you need me to do what I do," Harrison said before they walked off together in the direction of Mariella Marshall, who looked amazing in an emerald-green sheath dress.

The gentlemen's conversation was puzzling. What did they think Harrison could do to help and why would Jack pay him for that help? Jonas had noted something similar when he'd gotten Cath the appointment in Malibu. Weird, Kat thought. So weird.

"What are you doing, Kat?"

Kat snapped her head up at the words and looked into Jonas's handsome face and amused eyes.

"Hiding out," Kat told him, placing her hand in

the one he offered her, allowing him to draw her out of her hiding place.

"Are we that bad?"

"No. Not bad, it's just that remembering all the names and answering all the questions is exhausting." Thc warmth of his hand sent sparks up her arm. How those sparks ended up between her legs, God only knew.

"Tess is having fun," Jonas said.

Kat looked across the ballroom to see her friend, in an ice-blue gown, openly flirting with the very married mayor of San Luis Obispo. Tess was reveling in the attention she was receiving as the BFF of Jonas's lovc-at-first-sight fiancée, openly and gaily telling everyone that of course she'd known Jonas and Kat were dating, that she and Kat were exceptionally close.

"I guess I should go to the rescue," Kat said as the mayor's hand landed on Tess's hip.

Tess tossed her hair and lowered her eyes, going into full flirt mode. Oh, dear, trouble was on its way.

"She doesn't need rescuing," Jonas told her, placing his arm around her waist, his mouth resting against her temple. He'd been super affectionate all night and Kat had to keep reminding herself that it didn't mean anything, that it was all an act to sell their story.

"I was talking about rescuing the man she's flirting with."

Jonas laughed and the deep rumble caused her hormones to jump to their feet and start to boogie.

"He's harmless. Besides, his older, rich wife keeps a beady eye on him and will break up the cozy tête-à-tête soon enough. You, however, need to dance with me."

"I do?" Kat asked as he pulled her to the small dance floor in the middle of the room.

"You do. It's expected."

Damn, Kat thought as Jonas placed his hand on the small of her back and guided her into a smooth two-step. And here she was hoping he wanted to dance with her because he wanted his hands on her as badly as she wanted to put her hands on him.

It's an act, a con, a story you need to sell. It is not real life. If you carry on thinking like this, you're going to get your heart smashed!

A smashed heart hurts like hell, remember? If you don't, then we should spend some time recalling the tears, the humiliation, the feeling of being stabbed in the heart, over and over again.

You only get to be that stupid once in your life, Kat.

As per her directions, Jonas pulled his SUV into Cath's driveway. Kat watched as he walked around the big car to open her door. Kat saw the twitch of curtains in the front room and smiled. Cath was sitting in her favorite chair, anxiously awaiting their arrival. Having missed out on attending their engagement party, Cath wanted to meet the man of the hour. Since hearing about the engagement, Cath had asked Kat on a daily basis to bring Jonas by. Jonas easily, and readily, agreed to meet Cath, but finding the time when both Kat and Jonas were free had turned out to be a challenge.

She worked odd hours and Jonas worked long hours, and days could go by without them meeting or even talking. Such was the life of two fake-engaged people, Kat thought as Jonas opened the door for her.

Her hand slid into his and she sighed as those sparkles danced over her skin. She looked up and into his beautiful green eyes and her heart, predictably, stumbled. Thanks to her job she was immune to the power of gorgeous eyes in a handsome face and a hard body, but Kat noticed everything about Jonas—his strong tanned neck, his broad, ring-free hands, the tiny scar on his bottom lip—and was attracted to every inch of him.

And she had yet to see him naked. Damn, she was in so much trouble.

Their attraction was a living, breathing entity and when they came within twenty feet of each other, the urge to throw off their clothes was a constant temptation. She suspected that was why they'd, since the engagement party, used their busy schedules as an excuse to avoid each other.

Sex, they'd both agreed, was not part of the deal. It was a complication they did not need.

But she still, desperately, wanted to know what making love with Jonas felt like. Kat wondered if Jonas lay awake at night fantasizing about what they'd do to each other. She hoped so. She'd be pissed if she found out he was getting a solid eight and she was a hot mess of horniness.

Kat climbed down from the car and tipped her head to the side. “Don’t look now, but we are being watched.”

Jonas kept his eyes on her face and the corners of his mouth tipped up. “Then we should give your aunt something to see.”

Jonas cupped her face in his big hands, placed his thumbs on her jaw and dropped his mouth to meet hers. *Yes...this.* His lips were hard and masculine and, damn, so skilled.

Kat immediately forgot this was a demonstration kiss, a way to reassure her aunt that she was happy and in love. She fell into the moment, the rest of the world fading away. Her senses amplified and Kat could feel the prickle of warm sun on her back. With every breath she remembered to take, she inhaled traces of Jonas’s cologne. And his mouth was a revelation—a whisper and a storm, a fervent prayer and a banshee’s howl. It was heat and comfort and excitement and danger and home…

Confusion.

She wanted him. But she didn’t want to want him.

Kat stepped back, pushing her hand into her hair. She saw her own confusion echoed in his eyes. She touched her fingertips to her lips and Jonas’s eyes followed her movements. She knew that if she gave him the slightest hint, the smallest encouragement, he would kiss her again.

Strip her naked and slide on home.

But hopefully not on her aunt's lawn.

That little bit of silliness brought her back to where they were and what they were doing. Kat started to walk up the driveway, pulling her fractured thoughts together. How would Cath be today? She would be alert, she always was, but the length of their visit depended on Cath's levels of pain. Right now her doctor and caregiver were managing and monitoring the pain. There wasn't anything more they could do. Within the week Cath would be transported, by private ambulance provided by the clinic, to Whispering Oaks and she would be put on a new medical regime. Hopefully the new cocktail of drugs would provide an immediate improvement.

But that was for the future. Right now Kat had to convince her eagle-eyed aunt that she was madly in love with a sexy billionaire. Not so hard to do, Kat realized.

"So, Cath thinks you swept me off my feet," Kat told him as they approached the front door. Only her aunt would paint her front door that virulent shade of raspberry.

"Interesting color," Jonas said, his tone bland.

"She's an interesting woman," Kat replied, using her key to open the front door. "I wish you weren't meeting her when she feels so unwell. In her prime she was funny and loud and off-the-wall. Most afternoons my friends and I would end up at her house, just to hang out with her. She was…well, cool. She was everything my stepmother wasn't."

"Meaning?"

Kat shut the door behind her and kept the palm of her hand on the doorknob. She hadn't meant to say so much, but with Jonas, the words tended to flow out of her mouth without much thought. "June, my evil stepmother, was uptight, very concerned about what people thought about her. What they thought about her home, her marriage, her stepchild. My father did everything possible to make her happy and that included living far beyond their means. My home was filled with tension. This place was filled with love, acceptance and laughter. Here I could just…be."

Jonas took her hand, his long fingers linking with hers. "I'm glad you had Cath in your life."

Kat darted a quick glance at his face and noticed sadness in his eyes. "I know that your mother left you when you were a baby, but did you have a Cath in your life?"

Jonas looked past her to an oil painting on the wall behind her head. "I wasn't that lucky."

"I'm sorry," Kat whispered, wishing she had the courage to hug him, to offer comfort even though she knew he would not appreciate the gesture.

"Hey, you two, get in here! Stop kissing in my hallway!"

Kat rolled her eyes, turned away from Jonas and crossed the hallway to walk into the sunroom. Cath, her dark hair turned gray and cut super short after her bout of chemo, sat in the armchair by the window, her tablet on her lap.

She'd lost more weight, Kat immediately noticed, and it was weight she could not afford to lose. Kat placed her hands on the arms of the chair and bent to kiss Cath's cheek. "We were not kissing in the hallway," she told her aunt, sotto voce.

"Why not? He's a great-looking man. Is he a good kisser?" Cath demanded, laughter in her blue eyes and coating her voice.

Kat narrowed her eyes at her namesake. "Behave yourself, Catherine."

"Well, am I?" Jonas asked from the doorway.

Cath laughed and Kat thought it had been a while since she'd heard genuine amusement in her aunt's voice. Kat was grateful to Jonas for making Cath laugh, but the question made Kat blush. He was an amazing kisser. They both knew that. Just as they both knew that if they got naked they would leave scorch marks on the sheets. Or on the wall. The floor.

It was time to get off that topic, so she deliberately ignored his question. "Cath, meet Jonas Halstead. Jonas, Cath Long. Cath and my mother were identical twins."

"I was the prettier one," Cath told him as Jonas crossed the room to take the frail hand she lifted.

"That, I can believe." Jonas took both her hands in both of his. "It's so nice to meet you."

"It's much nicer to meet you," Cath told him and nodded at the chair next to her. "Take a seat. Let me get to know you."

Kat sat on the arm of Cath's chair as Jonas lowered his long body into the chair. "Cath, you promised not to interrogate him."

"I promised not to grill him. I didn't say I wouldn't ask him any questions."

Kat groaned. "Oh, God."

Jonas stretched out his long legs and rested his linked hands on his flat stomach, looking utterly relaxed. Damn him. "Relax, Katrina. I'm pretty sure I can answer any question your aunt throws at me."

"I like him already," Cath said. "Why are you marrying her?"

Kat held her breath as she waited for his response, staring hard at the frayed hem of her jeans. *If you tell her that you are in love with me, Cath will see through the lie.* "Because I think she's the most interesting woman I've met in a long time."

Kat lifted her head and her gaze slammed into his. That was the truth, she realized. He did think she was interesting. And that was…well, *interesting.*

"Are you going to buy her a new car?" Cath demanded, changing course.

"I'm trying to, but your niece is stupidly stubborn. I've run a few options past her but she keeps refusing them."

"Two sports cars and a high-end sedan," Kat snorted. "Too big and too expensive."

Cath leaned forward, ignoring Kat's statement. "I know how stubborn she is. It's so annoying! She hates asking for help. She sees it as a weakness."

Kat felt a headache building at the base of her neck. "Cath! Really?"

"Don't 'Cath! Really?' me," Cath retorted.

Kat looked at Jonas and saw that he was trying

not to laugh. Yep, he and Cath were now in cahoots, damn them.

"And have you persuaded her to give up her job and go back to school?"

"Working on it," Jonas answered her, keeping his eyes on Kat's face.

Kat lifted a warning finger. "Don't start."

"You really should do that, Kit-Kat. You can get your degree and then you can do what you want to do for a change."

"Which is?" Jonas asked, leaning forward.

Kat looked from his expectant face to Cath's smiling face and back to Jonas again. If she didn't tell him, Cath would. "I know that you'll probably think this is a line, that I'm saying this to impress you—"

"If you are, then it would be a first," Jonas smoothly interjected.

Kat wrinkled her nose at him. "I'd really like to do what you do. Projects. Developments. Building or renovating something. If I had lots of cash, then that's what I'd do."

Cath glanced from Kat's face to Jonas's, her eyes brimming with excitement. "Maybe after you are married, Jonas can bring you into the business. She's smart, Jonas, so smart."

Jonas's deep green gaze didn't leave Kat's face. "I know she is, Cath. Brains and beauty, it's a killer combination."

Kat tipped her head to the side. The problem with being smart was that she knew what was hidden beneath the words people said—or beneath the words they didn't say. Like sex, working with Jonas would never happen.

The image of her and Jonas working together flashed in her head and Kat smiled. She could easily imagine them arguing, then laughing, then arguing again. But, like making love, like their marriage being anything more than a business arrangement, it would never happen and she shouldn't let her imagination fly away with her.

Life didn't work like that.

Cath changed the subject and Jonas turned his attention to her. Cath, enjoying the conversation, peppered Jonas with questions about his childhood, his education, his hobbies and interests. Kat sat and listened and absorbed.

Her father would've liked him, Kat realized. He would've liked Jonas's no-nonsense way of speaking, his lack of snobbery. Wes, on the other hand, had always needed to point out to the world that he was someone, that he was successful.

Her father, like Kat, would've appreciated Jonas's don't-give-a-damn-what-you-think attitude. She could really like him, Kat thought. She could like him a lot.

If she let herself.

Needing to put some space between them, Kat stood. "I'm just going to say hello to Moira. She's Cath's caregiver."

"Bring Jonas back a cup of coffee when you return, darling." Cath patted her arm. "Jonas will stay here and we'll get acquainted."

What had they been doing for the past fifteen

minutes? Kat placed her hands on her hips and glared down at her aunt. "Behave yourself."

"Pfft." Cath waved her away.

Knowing this was a fight she couldn't win, Kat walked toward the door, praying Cath wouldn't bring out the photo albums. If she did, Kat was out of there.

Kat was about to walk into the hall when Jonas called her name. Keeping her hand on the frame of the door, she turned to look at him.

"You didn't answer Cath's question."

Kat frowned, puzzled. "What question?"

The mischief in his gaze, the crinkle around his eyes suggesting laughter, the fact that his mouth tipped up at the corners—all of that—should've given her a clue he was about to torpedo her. "You didn't tell her whether I was a good kisser or not."

Cath's laughter filled the room. Kat flushed and tipped her face up to look at the ceiling. When she looked at Jonas again, all amusement had fled from his expression. He seemed desperate to know the answer to his question. How could he not know that his touch made her burn? That he just had to look at her and her inhibitions, and common sense, melted away.

Saying he was a good kisser was like saying Michelangelo was an average painter.

Kat lifted her fingers to her lips, recalling the feel of his mouth on hers. She had to answer him, but how? How did she tell him that no one had ever managed to take her breath away until him? That he just had to sit in a worn chair and look at her and she couldn't find any air to inhale? His kisses were magical. His arms felt like home. His voice made her feel undone.

Kat opened her mouth to say something, even though she had no idea what words her tongue was trying to form, but before she could speak she heard the jovial voice of Cath's caregiver behind her. "Kit-Kat! I've been reading about your engagement in the society pages! So exciting!"

Kat pulled her gaze away from Jonas's and turned around to walk into Moira's hug. But, unfortunately, Moira's ample bosom didn't muffle Cath's sassy comment.

"Oh, you two are going to drive each other crazy. What fun!"

Not surprisingly Cath's definition of fun and Kat's own were wildly different.

Eight

Kat sat on the edge of Cliff House's wraparound third-floor balcony, her arms on the railing and her feet dangling off the concrete. Jonas had asked her to meet him there, and when she'd arrived he'd taken her on a tour of the once iconic hotel. He'd explained to her, in great detail, his plans for restoring the hotel. He'd seemed to enjoy having her input, encouraging her to make suggestions and really listening when she spoke.

She'd been hesitant to share her ideas at first, but when she forgot that he was a billionaire developer and she was a restaurant hostess, their conversation turned lively and engaging. It had been so nice to have a conversation that didn't involve celebrities and table seating and wait times and overindulged guests.

God, she wanted to do this, to do what she loved. And speaking of her future plans, she was going to have to postpone the writing of her LCA exam. With her crazy life as the Cinderella Bride of California's Hottest Billionaire—as she was now being called by the tabloid press—she hadn't even glanced at her books. If she sat for the exam now, she would fail and her time and money would be wasted. Dealing with Jonas, working at the restaurant and dodging the intrusive and downright annoying paparazzi left little time and energy for studying.

Kat felt her phone vibrate and she pulled it out of the back pocket of her denim shorts. She opened the text message and saw that Tess had sent her a link to a website. Tess found Kat's current celebrity status hysterical and kept track of the more outrageous stories about Kat and Jonas.

Kat clicked on the link and raised her eyebrows at the headline that appeared on her small screen: How an Average Santa Barbara Restaurant Hostess Snagged a Billionaire. Follow These Ten Easy Steps!

Kat rolled her eyes and scrolled down. "Step one. You've got to be where the rich men are. Kat Morrison works as a hostess at the fantastically exclusive El Acantilado restaurant and we bet that's where she plotted to snag Jonas's interest."

Kat rolled her eyes. What rot. Refusing to read any more, she was about to close the web page when she saw a link to an article titled "The Younger Marshalls, West Coast Royalty."

Kat skimmed the article probing into the love

lives of Harrison Marshall's children. Apparently Dr. Luc, the prominent plastic surgeon, was keeping company with Rachel Franklin, a congressman's daughter. Daughter Elana was still linked with a very married Hollywood producer, Jarrod Jones.

There was a picture of stylist son Rafe walking with a handsome man in Calistoga, their fingers brushing. The article went on to speculate on who Rafe's companion was. Why did it matter and who cared?

Fame, Kat thought, had never been so easy to achieve as it was these days. She was now semi-famous herself, simply for becoming engaged to a rich man. The Marshall children were famous because they were the offspring of America's favorite chef. It was crazy, Kat thought, that so many people were utterly fascinated by what the rich and famous, or infamous, did.

Kat felt Jonas's hand on her shoulder and was surprised when he sat beside her, his designer pants on the dusty balcony, his feet dangling off the edge. In front of them the Pacific Ocean was a perfect mix of blue and green and the setting sun tossed confetti sunbeams on the water's surface. The end of the day was approaching and soon the hotel would be empty of construction workers and she and Jonas would be its only occupants.

"I spoke to my project manager about changing that flooring in the ballroom as per your suggestion and he said it's doable. It's a cheaper option, also a lot less labor intensive so we'll save both time and money. This project is already over budget and running out of time, so I appreciate your input."

Kat felt pleasure, warm and delightful, unfurl inside her at his compliment. "You're welcome."

"You've got a good brain, Kat," Jonas said, his voice quiet. "You should be completing your degree so you can use it. Our marriage could give you that opportunity."

Kat rested her arms on the railing and pushed her chin into her wrist. It was such a lovely evening and she didn't want to argue with him. She just wanted to sit there, soaking in the late-afternoon sun, her shoulder and thigh against his, smelling the sea and watching the waves kiss the shore.

"I don't want to argue with you, not tonight."

"Then don't argue, just listen."

Kat waited for Jonas to speak, turning her head to look at his profile. His sunglasses were pushed up into his hair and soft stubble covered his cheeks. Like her, he looked tired, played out. This project was sucking up his time and, from a few other discussions they'd had—Jonas was remarkably forthright with her about the inner workings of his business—he was putting out fires all over the country. There was a delay on a project in Toronto, one of Halstead's directors was in the hospital after a heart attack and a major investor had just pulled out of a deal to build a new casino in Reno.

Jonas was also preparing to marry a woman he didn't love for reasons he'd never properly explained.

Oh, she knew about him losing his inheritance, but Kat suspected that there was more to the story.

"I actually respect the fact that you are independent, that you've gotten to where you are by your own effort. I sometimes envy the fact that no one can question whether you did it by yourself or not. People assume I am the CEO of Halstead & Sons because of Jack. Where else would a Halstead be? There is no doubt that you can do this, that you can hold your own."

There was a but coming…

"But, dammit, Kat, you make life so hard on yourself. You're exhausted, stressed, mentally and physically played out. And when I notice that, I get pissed because I can, with very little effort, lighten your load. You seem to treat this deal as if you are the only person benefiting from it, but this is a two-way street. I need you as my wife as much as you need my money."

"Will you tell me why?"

Jonas caught and held her glance, his eyes steady. "I might. If you consider taking a little more help from me."

"What sort of help?" Kat asked, suspicious.

"I'll cover Cath's medical expenses as agreed, but I'll also cover your current expenses and your studies. That way you can give up your job but still have income coming in. I'll give you a credit card you can use for emergencies. I know you won't use it but it'll make me feel better if you have it."

Kat hesitated, a part of her wanting to say yes but

so damn scared that she'd take this deal and then he'd rescind on his promises. She'd been burned by empty promises before. "I don't know, Jonas. You're asking a lot."

"I'm asking you to let me help you," Jonas replied, his voice calm and steady.

"I don't accept help easily."

Jonas released a small smile. "Yeah, I kind of realized that. Why not? Your ex?"

Kat nodded. "I went into our marriage as blind as a bat. He said he wanted to marry me, that he wanted to take care of me, that he loved me. I believed him."

Kat felt Jonas's eyes on her face but kept staring at the ocean, not wanting to see pity. "The first month we were married, the first time we had to pay our bills, he told me he expected me to pay my way. He said that if I wanted this marriage, and him, I'd show him how much I loved him by being an equal partner. All our living expenses were split exactly fifty-fifty. Well, I paid fifty percent of the mortgage but his name was on the deed. I paid money toward his car but he didn't pay anything toward mine. When I tried to argue my case, he withdrew and became icy cold. Being shut out like that was torture."

"I understand. My father was a master at that. He started freezing me out as a punishment, but soon his icy reserve turned into a habit. By my teens I'd learned not to care."

Kat heard the pain in his voice and touched his hand in comfort. He didn't pull away so she continued her story. "I wanted us to be happy, for him to be happy, so I acquiesced. To give Wes what he wanted, I had to work two jobs, one of them at El Acantilado."

"What a douche," Jonas said, his voice filled with outrage.

"I should've left him, but I wanted the marriage to succeed so I worked and studied and scraped up enough money each month to meet his terms. Then he complained that I wasn't spending enough time with him. I couldn't win. Then my dad died and, as I told you, everything went to my stepmom. I couldn't pay for school and I asked Wes to help me but he refused. Cath stepped up with the cash but Wes still expected me to pay exactly what I had been paying, between school and his demands, I was financially squeezed. Then came the ring incident..."

"What ring incident?"

Kat swallowed, the hurt as sharp today as it had been four years ago. "The only item I had of my mom's was an art deco ring, a square-cut sapphire surrounded by rectangular-cut diamonds. Not big or terribly valuable but it was given to her on her twenty-first birthday and my dad gave it to me on my twenty-first birthday. It had both mine and my mom's initials engraved on the band."

It hurt to talk about this but she needed Jonas to understand. "I had a car payment due and I couldn't swing it. It was the second one I'd missed and they were threatening to take my car. Wes kept some cash at home and I was desperate so I borrowed the money, leaving an IOU in its place. A few days later, I looked in my jewelry box and saw that my ring was gone. I confronted Wes and he told me that I had no right to take his money and that he'd replaced it by selling my ring on the internet. He said he hoped I'd learned my lesson. Three hours later, my stuff was packed up and I was living with Cath.

"That ring was the only link I had to my mom and he treated it like it was a used appliance, like it was nothing important," Kat whispered, feeling the all-too-familiar waves of grief, pain and mistrust. "I still check internet sites, hoping someone has put it up for sale, but no luck. It's futile, but I keep trying, hoping to find it."

"Give me your ex's name and address and I swear I'll make his life a living hell," Jonas said, his voice low with anger. "After I rip his head off and shove it where the sun doesn't shine."

Kat smiled at the image before sobering again. "Thanks to him, and to my dad, as well, I have a hard time trusting people. I can't rely on anyone to keep their word."

"I'm not him, Kat. I'm not going to change my mind. I'm not going to offer my support and then withdraw it, leaving you floundering. I mean what I say and I follow my words with actions. I know you find trust difficult, but you can trust that."

She wished she could. She wanted to. But her lack of trust was now a habit that would take time to change. "Anyway, getting back to your generous offer... Can I think about it? Can we talk about this again?"

Jonas's expression was pure determination. "And

we will." He pulled out his wallet, flipped it open and withdrew a card. He tucked it into the back pocket of Kat's jeans and when she opened her mouth to argue, he lifted his eyebrows. "No, we're not arguing about this. You run into a problem, you use the card. The rest of my offer we can discuss later but I need to know you have some sort of backup plan."

"I—"

"Change the subject, Kat."

Kat knew she wouldn't win this argument. Okay, so she had one of his credit cards, but she was never going to use it so arguing about it was pointless. She'd just leave it in her purse unused until he asked for it back.

Kat unfolded her arms and echoed Jonas's actions, placing her hands on the concrete behind her and leaning back.

"So, if you don't marry, Jack will disinherit you," she said, changing the subject and putting the spotlight on him. It was his turn to open up and Kat wondered if he would.

"Yep. I'll be out in the cold," Jonas replied, sounding remarkably sanguine.

"You make it sound like that doesn't bother you, but since you're prepared to take the drastic step of marrying me, I know that's not true."

"I'm not scared of starting over, of doing my own thing, of building something new," Jonas told her. "In fact, that would be awesome."

"It would?"

"Sure. It would be all mine, built with my own

sweat and tears, knowing that I was a hundred percent responsible for its success or failure. There's a freedom in that, Kat."

He sounded wistful, Kat realized, and she had an inkling of how being born into a legacy, as part of a successful clan, might mess with your head.

"Yet you are still marrying me to inherit your grandfather's shares."

"Yep. Loyalty to family is a bitch."

Kat cocked her head. "You once said to me that it was more important to you to keep the shares out of someone else's hands. Your dad's?"

Jonas looked shocked at her guess and even if he said nothing else, gave no further explanations, she'd know by his expression that she'd hit the nail on its head.

"What happened to cause such a rift between you two?"

Jonas stared at the beach far below them, his neck and back muscles tense. "What makes you think we have issues?"

"When I heard you speak to him at the engagement party, your voice changed. You were trying too hard to show the world, your grandfather, that you didn't hate Lane. He was a little better at concealing his loathing for you, but it was there. What happened?" Kat asked.

Jonas linked his hands behind his neck, his biceps bulging. "I was working my way up the ladder and Jack was CEO, but my dad, who was the chief financial officer, was making a lot of the decisions.

Because I wanted to prove to them both that I was as good as them, I was working sixteen, eighteen, hours a day, moving from department to department. I was working in the finance department at the time and Jack told me to analyze the books. Using my fancy degree, he wanted me to tell him where we were wasting money and how we could improve the bottom line. My father knew what I was doing but, not having quite the same attention to detail and work ethic as I do, didn't expect me to dig as deep as I did."

Kat lifted her hand to her mouth, immediately knowing where he was going with the story. "You found something—"

Jonas released a harsh laugh. "I found at lot of things. Kickbacks, siphoned funds, fake companies. He did it all and sucked millions out of the company coffers."

Kat felt sick. "Oh, Jonas. So what did you do?"

Jonas lifted one shoulder in a hard shrug. "I did what I needed to do to save the company. I told him to resign or else I would expose him and charge him with fraud. I told him if he did go quietly, then I'd keep his treachery from Jack. He could also keep his position as a Halstead director and the enormous salary that came with it, but if he ever opposed me, on anything, I'd expose him. I had him between a rock and a hard place, and because I had so much proof, he agreed."

"That must have been such a hard thing to do, Jonas. I've read articles written about Jack and I know he's a stickler for loyalty, demanding it from his employees and his suppliers. Loyalty to your grandfather or loyalty to your dad—you must've felt like you were being ripped apart."

Jonas slowly nodded. "I did. He resigned. I stepped into his position and went on to become the CEO. He still blames me for edging him out of the company. He acts as if I was desperate for the job, desperate to worm my way into Jack's good graces."

"He stole from the company!" Kat cried.

"Yeah, he's conveniently forgotten that part of the story," Jonas said, his voice as dry as bone.

"But why did he steal? It's not like you Halsteads are short of money."

"Gambling. He was addicted. That was another part of the deal I made with him. He left the company and he got treatment. He just transferred his obsession with cards into an obsession with art. As long as he stays far away from Halstead & Sons, he can do whatever the hell he likes with his money."

Kat bit the inside of her lip, still confused. "I still don't understand how this links with you having to marry."

Jonas rubbed his hand over his lower face. "Oh, that. Jack said that if I don't marry he's going to give his shares to Lane. If he does that, then Lane will have controlling interest of Halstead and he could cause a lot of trouble if he decided to resume his duties. One of two things could happen. I'd get fired and he'd have carte blanche to raid the company of its assets or I'd murder him and be sent to jail and then he'd raid the assets."

"Neither would be a good outcome."

"I want this company, Kat. I want people to look at it, and me, with respect again."

"They do," Kat protested.

"To an extent. But Jack's ruthlessness and my father's cutting-corners attitude are remembered. I want our name to be trusted. To do that, I need complete control, hence my need for a wife." Jonas stood, dusted his hands off on his pants and held out a hand to haul Kat up. "Do you know what else I need?" he asked when she was on her feet.

Desire replaced the bleakness in his eyes and Kat found herself edging closer to him, wishing she could follow up their conversation with a hug. She wanted to comfort him but she also wanted to feel that hot, hard, muscled body pressing into hers. Her breasts flat against his chest, his thigh between her legs, hands on her butt, mouth teasing hers.

"What?" She forced the word out, conscious of her pounding heart.

"Food. And sex." And there it was, what they both wanted but couldn't, shouldn't, have. "But that's still off the table, right?"

Nodding her head in agreement was one of the hardest things she'd ever done. After they'd both opened up emotionally, she wanted to be with him physically even more than before. But she managed to agree that they should abstain, with great reluctance. It was the smart thing to do and she prided herself in being a smart woman.

Jonas muttered a quiet curse and led her into the

old hotel. "Damn. Let's get some food. Then I'm taking you home, you're going to pack a bag—you don't need much, just shorts, tees and a swimsuit—and we're going to the airport. Do you have a passport?"

"Yes…" When his words sank in, Kat stopped walking. "A bag? Airplane? Passport? Where are we going? I can't go anywhere!"

Jonas just looked at her, still handsome in the shadows of the building. "Why not? You're not working this weekend and you need a break. I'm giving you one."

"B-but—" Kat spluttered. "I need to—"

"Cath is at the clinic and can't have visitors until the end of next week. You don't have any pets, nor do you have any obligations. Come with me to Saint Kitts, I need to check on a development there. It'll take an hour tomorrow morning, maybe two, and then we can spend the rest of the weekend doing absolutely nothing."

Oh, it sounded like heaven.

"Just say yes, Kat. Don't think, don't analyze, just say yes," Jonas said, his deep voice washing over her.

"Yes, okay. Let's go to Saint Kitts." Kat wondered who this woman was who was speaking on her behalf.

Was she crazy? She had obligations. She was supposed to be staying away from temptation so she didn't sleep with this too kind, way too sexy billionaire. She was Katrina Morrison and she didn't make impulsive decisions to jump on her fake fiancé's jet to head for the Caribbean at the last minute.

But, apparently, today she was that woman.

* * *

Jonas, Kat at his side, stood on the ridiculously green, springy and expansive front lawn and looked at the 18th-century restored sugar plantation. He liked the property, with its landscaped gardens and breathtaking ocean views, but he wasn't sure if he liked it enough to add it to the Halstead portfolio. The inn was turning a profit, but that wasn't good enough.

Kat, dressed in white shorts and a blue-and-white-striped cotton shirt with the sleeves rolled up, flipped through the folder he'd handed her to read. It contained financial statements, assets registers and sales forecasts…everything he needed to make a decision on whether to shell out a hefty chunk of change for the property.

"What do you think?" he asked Kat. "Should I buy it?"

Kat held the folder to her side and slowly turned in a circle, taking in the gray-and-white building with its wraparound balconies, the view of the cloud-shrouded mountain, the gardens and the amazing view of the water. When she stopped, a tiny frown appeared between her arched eyebrows. "It had a major restoration three years ago—roof, plumbing, pool, gardens. The rooms need redecorating and some of the furnishings need to be updated. The restaurant needs more experienced chefs. Most of the changes you'd need to do are cosmetic. But—"

She shrugged, deep in thought. "Those changes won't make a difference to the bottom line. Bookings are steady. The pricing is in line with what the other accommodation establishments are charging."

Her eyes lightened when she was excited and involved, Jonas thought. She loved this. She loved looking at the figures, making sense of them, matching the figures against the product. That big brain of hers was wasted as a restaurant hostess. Damn, if he wasn't going to marry her, he'd give her a job at Halstead tomorrow.

"I'd rebrand the property," Kat suddenly stated.

Jonas lifted his eyebrows. "You would?"

Kat nodded. "I'd spend money redecorating and reduce the number of rooms, make them bigger, more expansive, more luxurious and romantic."

"Less rooms, less income."

"Not if you charge a ridiculous amount for each room," Kat said, her voice rising in excitement. "I'd market this as a very luxurious wedding and honeymoon venue."

"There are other wedding venues on the island," Jonas pointed out, playing the devil's advocate.

"There isn't a venue with these views that will be this luxurious. I think it could work."

He did, too. It was a fantastic idea. Jonas took his phone from the back pocket of his jeans, dialed a number and kept his eyes on Kat. "Sian? Take a look at the plantation house on Saint Kitts. I want cost projections, payback periods, sales forecasts on what returns we'll get if we have to convert the place to a luxury wedding destination. Have the figures on my desk by Monday. Thanks."

Kat couldn't contain her wiggle of excitement. "Seriously? You think my idea has merit?"

He chuckled at her enthusiasm. "I think your idea has a lot of merit and that is why Sian is going to spend the weekend crunching numbers."

Kat winced. "That doesn't sound like fun for Sian."

"Sian gets paid a very hefty salary to do her job," Jonas replied. "Speaking of how to spend the weekend… Work is over. Let's start ours."

"All I'd like to do is lie on the beach, swim and lie on the beach some more," she said.

Kat shoved her hands into the back pockets of her jeans, her spine arching. The fabric of her shirt pulled over her small but perfect breasts and Jonas felt the blood draining from his head. So, maybe bringing her to the islands wasn't the smartest idea he'd ever have because… Crap. Sun and sea and sex went together like ice and cream. He'd managed, by the skin of his teeth, to resist her back in the States, so why had he thought he could do it here?

Inviting her to Saint Kitts had been impulsive, but they'd made a connection at Cliff House and he'd wanted to spend more time with her. He'd wanted to show her a place he loved. Obviously, if his brain had been working, he would've realized that Kat in a bikini would be more temptation than he could resist.

Kat fell into step beside him as they headed for the small parking lot and his rented, open-top Jeep.

"Where are we staying, by the way? Somewhere close to the beach?"

Jonas stopped, scanned the water and lifted his hand to point to a small island across a narrow straight. "We're going to Nevis. It's smaller than Saint Kitts, less commercial."

"Do you own a hotel there?" Kat asked as they resumed walking.

"I own a small house on Nevis. It's situated on a cliff and you walk to the end of the garden, down some wooden steps onto a private beach. It's isolated and quiet, and it's my favorite place in the world."

Kat stared at him, her eyes round. He could see the confusion in her eyes, the desire. She knew that being alone together would be dangerous, that there would be so many chances for them to end up in bed together. They were in the Caribbean, with warm seas, hot days and nights, minimal clothing. It wasn't rocket science.

Why had he risked inviting her again?

"Or," he said to give her a way out, maybe to give himself a way out, "we can stay here." He gestured to the house behind them. "The owners offered us two rooms for the weekend."

Please let me take you to my home. I need you.

Kat touched her top lip with her tongue, her eyes smoking over with heat. They both knew this was about more than a place he wanted to share with her.

If she said yes, they'd both be saying yes to much more than a temporary marriage.

"Let's go to your cottage," she eventually said, putting him out of his misery.

He had to make sure. For both of them. "I'm putting sex back on the table, Katrina. Do you understand that?"

Kat's blue eyes darkened. "On the table, on the beach, in a bed. It all sounds good to me. I'm tired of resisting what we both want."

Relief filled his chest. "Thank God. Okay, we need to head to the beach. I'm going to ask one of the local fisherman to ferry us across."

Kat's smile punched right through his gut. "What? No jet plane?"

"Impractical and expensive." Jonas returned her smile and slid his fingers around her hand. "Besides, crossing the Narrows in a boat is so much more fun."

They reached the rented Jeep and Jonas watched Kat climb up into the passenger seat, all long hair and longer legs. He wanted to taste her creamy skin, feel her amazing smile on his skin, get lost in the blue of her eyes. He'd wanted that for weeks. It was a testament to his determination that he'd held out this long.

He was finally, finally, going to make love to this amazing, vulnerable, smart, sweet woman. Jonas felt his heart stutter and stumble.

Do you know what you are doing, Halstead? She could mess with your head. This could go deeper than sex, could mean more than a weekend fling. She could become someone you want for more than a temporary marriage.

Jonas shook his head, hoping to dislodge his crazy

thoughts. *You've had flings before*, he told himself. *You know how to do this.*

Yeah, but he'd never had a fling with Katrina Morrison. She was different from anyone he'd ever met before. And she'd be moving in, as his *wife*, very soon.

Even so, he could handle this.

Maybe.

Nine

Kat, her mind churning, her body pulsating, allowed Jonas to lead her across the front porch with its 180-degree ocean views and into his charming and traditional Caribbean-style home.

Kat heard the thump of bags hitting the floor and watched as Jonas walked over to the windows and opened the shutters, allowing dappled sunlight and a cool breeze to enter the room, raising goose bumps on her skin.

Or the goose bumps could be because of the way Jonas was looking at her. Dressed in black cargo shorts, a hunter green T-shirt and flip-flops, he looked more like a surfer than a CEO, sexy enough to dissolve any second thoughts she had.

“Are you sure this is what you want?” Jonas asked.

"This is what I want." Kat forced the words past her dry lips. Jonas started to walk toward her but stopped when she lifted her hand. "This is what I want until we get back to Santa Barbara. This is what I want for the next two days. It might not be what I think is best later on. Is that okay?"

"Two days with an option to renew?"

She huffed a small and nervous laugh. "Exactly."

Jonas started walking toward her again.

Kat hadn't seen anyone this sexy for a long time. Okay, never. It had been so long since she'd had a lover…

So damn long.

Kat's hand flew up again and Jonas stopped a meter away from her. The jumping muscle in his cheek was the only indication of his frustration. "Yeah?"

"It's been a while," Kat said, feeling embarrassed. "I'm not on the pill and I don't carry condoms. Even worse, I don't know if I remember how to do this."

Jonas stepped closer and placed his hands on her hips. She noticed tenderness in his eyes. Man, she wanted—craved—some tenderness. "I know how to do this and I have protection. I'll make this good for you, Kat, I promise."

Kat nodded, her hands resting on his chest. Her heart felt like it was about to burst. "I know, but I don't know if it'll be good for you," she said, her soft words muffled.

Jonas tipped her chin up with his knuckle. "Sweetheart, you're in my arms and it's already amazing. Your kisses rock my world so I am not worried."

Jonas looked at her mouth, bounced his gaze up to hers and looked at her mouth again. "Any more questions? Because I'm dying here."

Jonas didn't wait for her answer. His mouth met hers and he didn't bother with soft and sweet, he just hurtled straight to demanding and desperate.

His tongue delved into her mouth, swirled, retreated and dived in again. His kiss was fine wine and Belgian chocolate, bungee jumping and coral sea diving. It was heat and happiness and hunger.

Kat loved being kissed by him, but she wanted more, so much more, so she pushed her hips into his, sighing when her stomach encountered the hard length of him.

Yeah, she wanted more.

Instead of dialing it up, Jonas stepped away from her, his fingers the only part of him touching her. He ran them down her cheek, over her jaw. What was the problem? Why was he stopping?

Kat didn't know she'd spoken the words aloud until Jonas answered her question. "I'm stopping because if I don't, I'm going to last two seconds and that's not how I want this to go."

"I can do fast," Kat assured him, already missing his hard body against hers, his mouth fused with hers.

Jonas shook his head. "Nope, it's not going to happen that way, Kit-Kat."

Kat's heart melted at hearing Cath's pet name for

her on his lips. It made her feel special, wanted, a little…loved.

No, this was sex, not love. *Don't you dare get the two confused, Kat.*

"Let's take this to the bedroom," Jonas said, bending his knees to hook an arm around the backs of her thighs. He lifted her and held her against his chest, easily carrying her across the room and down the hallway.

Kat played with his hair and nuzzled his jaw. In the bedroom, which was decorated in soft greens and white with a high ceiling, Jonas dropped her to her feet in front of a free-standing, white, wood-framed mirror.

He stood behind her, big and dark, his face a mask of concentration. His hands rested on her shoulders and Kat watched, fascinated, as his fingers danced over to the open V at her neck. Those big hands undid the buttons of her shirt, slowly revealing more of her skin to his hot gaze.

"Watch me touch you, sweetheart," Jonas commanded, his eyes blazing pure green fire.

When her shirt lay open he pulled it off her shoulders and down her arms, revealing her lacy white bra to his intent gaze. Jonas kissed the side of her neck as he cupped her breasts, easily covering them with his big, broad hands.

Kat lifted her arms and gripped the back of his neck, her arching back lifting her nipples into his palms. Jonas groaned and swiped his thumbs over the hard nubs.

"Look at your eyes," he said, his words a low growl in her ear. "Look how they go a deeper, darker blue. *So* sexy."

She flicked her eyes to her reflection but her attention was snagged by the look on his face. Passion and concentration, all his attention focused on her, his only aim to give her pleasure.

Jonas dropped his hands from her breasts and pulled back, and she felt the fastenings to her bra open. She tried to turn but Jonas held her against him, meeting her eyes again in the mirror.

"No, like this," he insisted. Slowly—so, so slowly—using one finger, he pulled one cup down, revealing her right breast, her nipple rosy and hard and begging to be touched, kissed. Jonas groaned, ground his erection into her lower back and yanked the bra off her, dropping it to the floor.

"Going slow is killing me," Kat muttered, moving his hands back to her breasts, silently asking for more.

"It'll be worth it, I promise." Jonas's hands skimmed down her breasts, over her flat stomach to dip beneath the band of her shorts. Kat covered his hands with hers, dragging her fingertips over the backs of his hands and up his wrists before snapping open her shorts and pushing the fabric down her hips and thighs to the floor.

Jonas whispered a low curse in her ear. Her gaze flew to his face but his attention was on the tiny triangle between her thighs. "You are so damn beautiful."

Kat looked at her body in the mirror, practically naked and standing in his arms. Her breasts were high, her stomach flat, her legs long. She looked the same as she always did, but not. She looked, she realized, animated, as if she was glowing from the inside out, as if Jonas had flicked on all the lights inside her.

She looked like a woman who was desperate for her lover's touch. And she was. She yearned to know his secrets, to taste his soul. All the worries and risks that had held her back before now seemed like nothing in the face of this desperation.

Jonas ducked his head, placed his open mouth on her neck and slipped his hand under the fabric of her panties, his finger unerringly finding her sweet spot.

Kat felt the sparks, then the bolts of lightning, the heavy heat in her womb.

She also felt peace, like this was right. Jonas touching her, pleasuring her, was the only thing she was supposed to be doing right now.

"God, Jonas…" Kat murmured. "That feels so good."

"I'm glad, honey."

Jonas pulled his hand from between her legs, spun her around and covered her mouth with his. Her panties slid down her legs and then Jonas was pushing two fingers back inside her and placing his thumb against her clit.

Kat wound her arms around his neck, holding on because her legs were no longer able to support her.

The white light behind her eyes intensified and

Kat pulled her mouth away, panting. "I'm so close. I need to come, Jonas."

She didn't care that she sounded crazy. She needed this release.

"Trust me, you will." Jonas looked around the room, smiled and walked her over to the windowsill, placing her bare butt on the cool wood. He shoved the shutters open and Kat felt the salty air on her skin, heard the waves crashing on the beach below. "Yeah, this will work."

Jonas dropped a hard kiss on her open mouth before reaching up and pulling his T-shirt over his head.

That chest, Kat thought, pushing her fist into her sternum. Wide, muscled, with a light smattering of hair that crossed ridged stomach muscles in a perfect line.

Her gaze dancing across his body, Kat held her breath as Jonas shucked his shorts and underwear. There he was, masculine, straight and hard. Kat lifted her hand to touch him but Jonas shook his head.

"Later. This is still about you."

"Me touching you is what I want," Kat murmured as he dropped to his knees in front of her, his wide shoulders pushing her thighs apart. Oh, God, it was too much, too intimate…

"Trust me, Kat."

She would. She did. Kat relaxed.

"I keep saying it but it's true. You are truly stunning."

No one had ever called her lady parts stunning. Kat had barely finished the thought when Jonas kissed her, his mouth on the most secret part of her. Embarrassment scuttled away as sensation swamped her. This was lovemaking like she'd never experienced before.

Jonas pulled back and sat on his heels, his big hands moving to her torso, his gaze scanning her body. Kat dropped her head back as his finger—that clever, amazing, lightning-infused finger—explored her belly button, went lower, touched her bead and slid into her hot, wet passage. Then a second finger joined the first, his tongue swirled around, and every inch of her body hummed.

His fingers curled into her as his mouth loved her and she flew away on fireworks of pleasure. Light—pure and pulsating—flashed behind her eyelids and her body tensed, every inch of her poised like a free diver on a cliff, a base jumper on a building's ledge. And then she was flying…

Feminine power rushed from a place deep inside her until a dazzling display of fireworks erupted from her innermost core. Pleasure swirled and twirled, each revolution less potent than the last until the whirlwind stopped and she could breathe again. Panting, she hunched over, a light sheen of sweat on her skin.

Jonas placed a light kiss on her inner thigh before sitting back on his heels to look at her.

"I never… I can't… Wow."

A long, slow, smile crossed Jonas's face. "Good?"

"Amazing. Thank you." Kat suddenly realized she was recovering from a hell of an orgasm and he was still rock-hard and waiting.

Jonas just looked at her, waiting for her to make the next move. They had yet to make love, she realized. The past fifteen minutes had been his gift to her. She wanted togetherness now. Oneness. The giving and receiving of physical love.

Kat stood, held out her hand and watched as Jonas rose, in one fluid movement, to his feet.

He took her hand, curling his fingers around hers. "You're mine until we land in Santa Barbara," he stated, his tone suggesting that she not argue.

"I'm yours," Kat agreed, holding his volcano-hot gaze. "So, are those condoms anywhere close?"

There was a wave behind her. She was lying face-down on the board and she was paddling. So far, so good. When she felt the board rise, she had to pop up—*Pretend you're doing a pushup*, Jonas had told her—she had to stand…now!

Kat pushed up, wobbled into a crouch and the board skittered out from under her as the wave crashed over her head. Spitting out a mouthful of briny water, she planted her feet in the sand and pushed her wet hair out of her eyes.

She sucked at surfing.

Kat turned around and watched Jonas fly down a wave. She pulled a face. Her fake fiancé and current lover did not suck at surfing. He looked as at home on a surfboard as he did in the boardroom, on a construction site, on top of her, sliding into her.

Of all the things Jonas did well—of which she knew there were many—making love to her, she was convinced, was what he was best at.

She loved being with him, spending time exploring their passion. Sex with Jonas was off-the-charts amazing. But Kat also enjoyed just being with him. Hanging out in his kitchen, watching him cook, which he, annoyingly, also did really well. Cuddling on the hammock strung between two trees, him reading while she lay with her head on his shoulder, watching the endless blue ocean. Easy conversation and teasing laughter, drinking red wine while walking on the beach at midnight.

They'd only been here a day or two, but she loved this life, so far away from the craziness of what they were doing in Santa Barbara. This island life was relaxed, uncomplicated and easy. Out of the glare of society and flashing cameras, away from the demands of his life as CEO of an enormous company and Cath's illness, Kat felt more like herself than she had for…so long. Years.

She liked the Nevis version of Kat. She really, really, liked this laid-back, Nevis version of Jonas, and she knew that if they weren't leaving tomorrow, if they stayed here, she'd fall in love with him.

Maybe she was a little, or a lot, in love with him already.

It couldn't go anywhere, though. They were marrying under crazy circumstances. She was marrying him for money. He was marrying her for control over his company's future. For a marriage to succeed it had to be based on love first and last; it couldn't be complicated by "if you do this, then I'll do that." As she knew, making a marriage work was tough enough before adding any extra complications.

Kat looked up at the cliff, picturing the house behind the trees. It was her dream house—small, cozy, compact. Simple. She could live a simple life with Jonas the Surfer.

A life with Jonas the CEO Billionaire would not be so straightforward.

Kat sat with the board between her legs, telling herself it was salt burning her eyes and not tears. She knew, thanks to her wretched marriage and her father's death, that not everything in her life would last forever, but this…

This overwhelming feeling of contentment she was experiencing bobbing on a clear Caribbean sea, watching her lover surf—this she wanted to keep forever. But life didn't work that way. She'd have to let this dream, this contentment, trickle through her fingers when they left Nevis behind.

Something would go wrong when she left the island, when they went back to reality. Of course it would. They couldn't have it all. Well, maybe Jonas could, but she couldn't. She was setting herself up for a big fall if she thought he'd solve all her problems. People lied. People misrepresented the truth. They changed their minds, changed their perceptions.

Nothing was cast in stone; everything could go

sideways on her. It was better to keep her distance, to keep scanning the horizon, to keep giving herself time to dodge those missiles that would blow up her life. This wasn't a fairy tale, Jonas wasn't her prince and she wasn't going to end up in a castle sipping mimosas for breakfast.

She didn't want to be a princess. She just wanted to protect her heart. Was that wrong?

Later, much later, when she and Jonas were over, when they'd both received what they'd needed from each other, when they'd fulfilled their bargain, she'd remember this moment. She'd remember this feeling of love and contentment seeping from every pore.

She'd remember and she'd smile, grateful she'd felt what it was like to be—mentally, physically, spiritually—in the right place, loving the right person, at least once in her life.

She'd remember. And she'd try not to mourn.

Kat plastered a smile on her face and walked into the ornate lobby of the Grenada Theater, silently cursing Jonas for asking her to meet him at the black-tie fund-raiser instead of picking her up at her apartment.

She recognized many of the attendees—many of them had dined at El Acantilado—but she didn't know them well enough to strike up a conversation.

Kat took a glass of champagne from a tray carried by a smartly dressed waiter. She lifted the cool glass to her lips as she moved to the edge of the crowd, putting her bare back against the wall and hoping Jonas would soon arrive.

He'd been delayed in Toronto and was running late, or so his text had said. Kat pushed away her doubt; Jonas didn't lie. If that's what he said happened then that's what happened. She couldn't keep allowing her past to influence her future, she thought. Jonas wasn't Wes…thank God. Her first husband and her almost-second husband were completely, utterly different.

Staring down at her gold sandals, Kat realized this would be their last formal engagement before their wedding a week from today, which would be under snow-white tents on fields at the Polo Club.

She was getting married…

To a man she'd barely knew and who she'd hardly spent any time with lately.

Jonas had made love to her twice on the flight home from Saint Kitts, but when the plane had landed on US soil, Jonas her sexy surfer disappeared and Jonas the CEO returned. Now, three weeks had passed since they'd loved, played and laughed in Nevis and, despite attending social events, he hadn't, not once, made an attempt to kiss her. Underneath the longing and lust, she was grateful. They couldn't go back. This was their real life. And if they attempted to recreate their time in Nevis, tried to relive their fun-filled days and nights, they'd tarnish the memory of that amazing weekend.

No, it was better this way. In Santa Barbara, Jonas and Kat weren't the same people who'd loved each other senseless in the Caribbean. To keep her heart intact, to get through the next week, their so-called honeymoon, the next year, they had to be different people. If she was lucky, they'd skate through their business-deal marriage with no major issues. If luck deserted her, then she'd deal with whatever came her way and soldier on.

It wasn't like she had a choice. Cath needed her to make it to the altar.

Nothing could go wrong now and nothing would. She and Jonas had a deal, well discussed and thought out. Each had a copy of the signed contract, for goodness sake! The only way the wedding could be derailed was if either of them bailed, and neither would. They had too much skin in the game.

"Kat."

Kat lifted her head and smiled at Sian, Jonas's assistant, glad to see someone she knew. "Hi. I'm so glad you're here."

"Jonas wanted to make sure that you got his message that his flight was delayed," Sian explained. Her gaze traveled up Kat's body and she twirled her finger, silently telling Kat to turn around. Kat complied.

"Now that's a hell of a dress," Sian said.

It was, Kat admitted. It was a shimmering gold, floor-length gown with an extremely thigh-high slit that exposed her legs. It plunged down the front and down the back, just skimming the top of her butt. Kat felt nearly naked but Tess, who was her self-appointed and bossy stylist, wouldn't allow Kat to wear anything else.

You and Jonas agreed that he would pay for the designer dresses you needed for formal occasions, and this special screening of Swan Lake *is black tie all the way. Wear the damn dress.* Tess had been wearing her don't-argue-with-me-or-I'll-hurt-you look, so Kat had worn the dress.

Without, as Tess had insisted, any underwear.

Pray to God that Kat didn't get into an accident on the way home.

"Oh, did you hear that Jonas bought the plantation inn you guys looked at in Saint Kitts?" Sian asked.

He did? Kat felt a knife pierce her heart, hurt that he hadn't told her he was going to buy the property. "Oh," Kat replied, looking down into the gold liquid in her glass. "That's nice."

"He's upgrading, per your suggestion, to a super-luxurious honeymoon destination. He also said you are a natural at property development and if things were different, he'd employ you tomorrow."

Oh, wow. That was a hell of a compliment. But the words would've meant so much more if he'd said them to her face.

Sian moved so she stood next to Kat, her back also to the wall. Now feeling more comfortable, they looked at their fellow guests, making chitchat and low comments on shoes and dresses they liked.

"Mariella Santiago-Marshall is wearing Gucci. I love the color on her. You have to be careful with that shade of tangerine."

Kat followed Sian's gaze and saw Harrison's wife, who looked amazing in a pink-and-orange sheath, her black hair pulled off her face and diamonds dripping from her ears and wrists. Mariella, her hand in Harrison's arm, looked around the room, caught

Kat's eyes and smiled at her, lifting her hand in a small wave.

"The Queen just acknowledged you," Sian said on a laugh. "And Jonas has finally arrived." Kat swung her head toward the door but Sian placed her hand on Kat's arm and her fingernails pushed into Kat's skin. "Whoa, look! Oh, I wonder what that's about."

Kat turned her gaze back to Harrison and Mariella. Harrison had turned away from Mariella, his broad shoulder blocking her view of his cell phone, a little smile on his face. If she hadn't been watching carefully, Kat would've missed the hurt and fear that crossed Mariella's face, the flash of anger at being dismissed and ignored.

Trouble in paradise? Maybe.

"That wasn't a business call," Sian said, still watching the Marshalls as Kat turned away to find Jonas.

Talking about trouble, six foot two of sexy was heading her way. Kat barely heard Sian's words because she was watching Jonas walk toward her, the crowds parting to get out of his way. He ignored the greetings of people he passed, his eyes never leaving Kat's face. Kat felt every inch of her skin heat; saw the passion and desire blazing in his eyes.

"Holy crap," Sian said from what felt like a place far away.

Kat looked into Jonas's intense expression and it was as if she could feel his mouth, his skilled lips, moving across her jaw, down her throat to pull a nipple between his teeth. Kat felt Sian take her glass from her hand and Kat placed both her palms on the wall behind her, hoping to support her shaky legs.

She could feel the heat in his eyes. She wanted to step into that desire and burn with him. Sian, the ornate red-carpeted lobby, the wrought-iron staircases, the elite of the West Coast faded away. Just she and Jonas remained, caught in a space and time that was solely their own.

Jonas reached her and, shielding her from the rest of the room, placed his index finger in the very low V of her dress and tugged.

"I blame your super sexy body and the memory of how you felt in my arms for my inability to concentrate. The memories of you, under me, me in you, have distracted me every minute of every day. I blame you entirely for my exceedingly low productivity these past few weeks.

"I want you," he added. "I've wanted you every minute since we left the islands and I'm damn tired of fighting it."

Kat swallowed, unable to look away, desperate to have his mouth on hers. She needed him, again. Now. "I know. I feel exactly the same way. Let's put sex back on the table." Kat placed her hand on the lapel of his jacket and felt the thud-thump of his racing heart through the fabric. "Take me home, Jonas. I want to be with you. I *need* to be with you."

Jonas gave her a hard nod, gripped her hand and led her through the now quiet lobby, ignoring the amused, shocked and envious looks directed their way.

She didn't care what they thought. Jonas, what he could give her and what she could give him—that was all that was important.

Ten

His limousine was still parked outside the theater, his driver sharing a quick smoke with one of the parking valets. Jonas, keeping Kat's hand in his, called his driver's name and the man sprang into action, running around the car to open the door. All the saliva left Jonas's mouth as Kat bent to climb into the car, the fabric of her dress clinging to every luscious curve. He realized she wasn't wearing any underwear and his semi-hard erection hardened to steel.

Jonas followed her into the car, issued a terse instruction to the driver to take him back to his hotel—it was closer than her apartment—and hit the button to bring up the privacy screen. He half turned and looked at Kat. He'd just pulled her out of a black-tie event and everybody there, his grandfather and

Harrison Marshall included, knew exactly how he intended to spend the rest of his night.

He didn't give a rat's ass. They could think what they liked. All he knew was that he'd been denying himself since their return from Nevis. And once he'd seen her there, he could no longer remember why. There was no way he could sit through *Swan Lake* with Kat's perfume in his nose without going slowly insane.

Jonas glanced at his watch. He'd managed three weeks, six days and eight hours without touching her and it was three weeks, six days and eight hours too long.

"Are you okay?" Kat asked, her voice soft and a little worried.

"I'm fine." Jonas ran the tip of his finger from the delicate V in her throat to the scooped edge of her dress. "This dress… Holy crap."

Kat sent him a look from under her eyelashes that was part wicked, part innocence and all hot. "Do you like it?"

"I think it's frickin' sensational." Jonas pushed the thin strap holding the triangle of fabric off her shoulder. One more swipe and her perfect breast lay bare. Jonas swallowed and, unable to resist, ducked his head to take her nipple into his mouth, lathing the responsive bud with his tongue. Fire licked a path from his mouth to his groin and blood pulsed into his dick, hot and hard. He felt Kat's hands in his hair, holding his head to her, heard her soft whimpers.

He pulled back, looked into her eyes and fell. Hard. "God, I've missed you."

"I've missed you, too. I miss Nevis," Kat said, her voice trembling, and he heard the truth in her words, felt them because he missed Nevis, too. He missed the simplicity they'd found there, the lack of drama.

Kat held the back of his neck, pulled his head down and her lips moved over his, at first hesitant and then more confident. Her hand slipped under his jacket, between the buttons of his shirt, to find his bare skin, as her agile tongue dipped into his mouth, sliding against his.

Possession, need, desperation flooded his system and he wanted more, needed her now. He couldn't wait. Jonas pushed his hands under the nearly indecent slit of her dress and pushed the expensive fabric up and over her smooth, bare hips. God, so sexy.

"Lift up," he muttered against her mouth, his hand on her butt. Kat lifted, the material bunched behind her and Jonas opened the snap to his trousers and pulled down the zipper. Before he could free himself, Kat's hands were in his underwear and his vision started to tunnel. He needed to get inside her.

Jonas looked out through the tinted glass, saw that the car was crawling along State Street and, if they hurried, they'd have time.

Slow and sexy would be for later, he needed to take the edge off.

"Jacket pocket, wallet, condom," he growled against her lips, his hand sliding between her thighs to check if she was as ready for him as he was for her.

Cash and cards dropped to the seat of the vehicle, his wallet bounced off the floor and Kat used her teeth to open the condom. Then, thank God, he felt the heat of her fingers on him as she rolled the latex down. As she finished, he gripped her waist with both hands and lifted her onto him. Kat squeaked as her hot core connected with his hard shaft and her eyes closed in an expression of bliss.

"Kit-Kat," he groaned as she slid her wet heat against him, "we don't have much time. We need to do this fast."

Kat gripped him in one hand, positioned him at her opening and pushed down at the same time as he launched his hips upward. Jonas's eyes flew open to check whether he'd hurt her, but Kat's eyes were fixed on his, her bottom lip between her teeth, her hands clutching the fabric of his shirt and she was riding him. Small movements, bigger movements, swirling around him in a dance that was part torture and all pleasure.

Torture and pleasure, that adequately described these past few weeks. Pleasure being with her, torture never being alone with her. He'd missed her, missed her more than the fantastic memory of great sex. He'd missed her laugh, her little frown that appeared when she was concentrating, her sexy laugh. When he was with her he felt calmer, stronger, better.

"Ah, sweetheart," Jonas muttered, lifting his hands to cover her breast, thumbing her nipples to give her as much pleasure as possible.

Kat responded by moving faster and Jonas, following where she led, pumped his hips. He needed her to come before he did but he had no control around this woman.

"Kat, I can't—"

Kat slammed down on him, her mouth an inch from his. "You don't have to." Jonas felt her clench around him, felt the ripples deep inside her.

Wrapping his arms around her to keep her still, he pistoned his hips, driving upward and into her, and felt like his head was about to spin away. His orgasm roared from his balls up his spine and into his brain and his vision faded.

This. Her. Kat.

He couldn't wait another three weeks—he couldn't wait another three damn hours—until they did this again.

Something had changed and shifted inside him somewhere between Nevis and the back of this car and, as a result, something had to change between them. He couldn't live with her, pretend to be her husband and not have her in his bed.

Something had to change, Jonas thought again as Kat rested on his chest.

He just wished he knew what.

Through the open doors leading to the balcony area of his penthouse suite, Jonas, lying in the huge bed with Kat draped across his chest, watched the first signs of a new day. The pinks and oranges of what promised to be an awesome sunrise broke through the night sky. Despite feeling exhausted from making love with Kat throughout the night, he'd been unable to sleep.

Jonas looked down at his lover, at the delicate hand on his chest, the colors of her fire opal echoed in the sunrise. He touched the ring with the tip of his finger, thinking that this wasn't how he wanted her to wear his ring.

This wasn't the way it was supposed to be.

Jonas gently picked up Kat's arm, placed it on her hip and pulled his other arm out from under her. He didn't want her to wake up, not yet. If she opened those amazing eyes he wouldn't be able to stop himself from taking her again. He needed time to think.

They'd attended a few social engagements together but he'd deliberately limited their alone time, thinking that he needed some time to work out what had happened between them in Nevis. Obviously he was wrong.

Kat rolled over and buried her face in his pillow. Jonas snagged a pair of running shorts from the chair next to his bed and pulled them on. He walked through the French doors onto the balcony, placed his forearms on the railings and looked out to sea.

Being fake engaged to Kat was killing him. The lies, the pretense—it was sucking away at his soul. Having that time in Nevis, when everything had felt so real, just made the pretense harder to pull off. He was so tired of manipulating and being manipulated, doing deals, considering the consequences of all his choices.

He'd spent the last fifteen years of his life dodging bullets, trying to live up to his grandfather's expectations, trying to keep the veneer of his family intact. Keeping his father's theft from his grandfather had been a stupid move, he now admitted. Lane did the crime; he should've had to face the consequences. Jack would've disinherited him, that much Jonas was sure of. Jack was intolerant of theft and couldn't stand disloyalty.

At the time, Jonas had thought he was protecting Lane, but really, he'd been scared to be the bearer of bad news. He'd thought that Jack might blame him, that Lane's decisions would impact Jonas and Jack's relationship. Jonas had also hoped that protecting his father would draw him and his father together, that Lane would feel grateful to Jonas for saving his skin. He'd hoped they'd finally be the father-and-son team he'd dreamed of in his childhood. It hadn't happened like that. His so-called help had just pushed them further apart.

Lane loathed him and Jonas understood why. When Lane looked at his son, he couldn't pretend that he'd left the company because he needed a new challenge, because he'd wanted to explore a world beyond that of Halstead & Sons. Jonas had seen Lane's dark underbelly and because Lane couldn't snow Jonas, he couldn't completely snow himself.

How could Jonas have ever thought they would forge a stronger relationship built on deceit, on theft, on disloyalty?

But wasn't he doing exactly the same thing with Kat? There was something between them, something powerful that was trying to form, but their foundation was rocky. Wasn't there an old Bible analogy about building your house on sand and not rock? That's what they were doing, building on sand…

In fact, his whole life was built on sand. It kept shifting for Jack's whims, and Jonas was so tired of shifting sands.

He wanted something different… But what?

Jonas stared at the rising sun, the bands of pink-and-orange ripples tossed on the sea, his mind running fast and hard.

What did he want? Halstead?

Yeah, he wanted the company. He loved what he did, but he wanted it free and clear, on his terms, no one else's. He wanted it if, and only if, Jack thought he was the best person for the job, only if Jack thought Jonas's track record as CEO warranted him taking over the company. If Jack was going to force Jonas into marriage and rule from the grave, he could take Halstead and shove it. Jonas had enough money of his own to walk away, to start again. He could renovate houses, do smaller developments, start off slow. He wasn't scared of hard work and, damn, he'd be free of the red tape and BS that went with dealing with Jack and the shareholders.

He also wanted Kat, in his life, in his heart, in his bed. But if he told her he wanted a clean break, that he wanted to live and work without the manipulation of Jack and the guilt of his past, that he wanted to live that life with her, she wouldn't believe him. Thanks to her moron ex, she wouldn't believe that he would keep his promise to pay for Cath's care, that he had more than enough to take care of them both and start a new company with Kat at his side.

He could walk away from Halstead, but if he bailed out of this deal with Kat, there would be consequences. He'd have to honor his debt to her; Cath was already at Whispering Oaks and she was making progress. Not much but some. There was hope. He couldn't jeopardize her treatment; that wouldn't be fair. He had the six million to honor his debt to Kat, too, but that wasn't the problem. The problem was her stiff pride.

She'd only agreed to this crazy deal because there was something in it for him, because he needed her as much as she needed him. If he tipped the scales, she would refuse to take his cash. She wouldn't let him pay for Cath's treatment.

If he backed out of their deal, she'd refuse to continue her studies. Kat would continue working at El Acantilado and it would take her forever to get her degree and move into a job she loved. He couldn't do that to her. She deserved to be happy. She could see the light and he didn't want to shove her back into darkness.

But he couldn't go through with the marriage as they'd set it up. He had to break the hold Jack had on him. He had to do that to survive, to regain his self-respect. That was something being with Kat had taught him. But he also had to make sure Kat was taken care of and to do it in a way she wouldn't reject.

He might lose her; he accepted that. But he'd had

honesty with her in Nevis, and he wouldn't settle for less. He'd rather lose this half-real situation now and hope they could start over than lose her forever because they hadn't built their relationship on truth. If they were meant to be together, if she loved him even a little, then they would find their way back to each other.

They would find their way back to each other. They had to, because if they didn't then he was properly screwed.

Jonas heard her soft footsteps behind him and sighed when she wrapped her arms around his bare waist and placed her cheek against his spine. Pushing his arms back, he held her hips, closing his eyes. How could he allow her to leave his life? How was he going to let her go? He didn't know. He just knew that he had to do it.

Kat placed an openmouthed kiss on his spine before sliding under his arm to face him, her back to the rising sun and the view. She was dressed in his button-down shirt, her dark hair and the white shirt a perfect contrast, her blue eyes still sleepy. Messy hair, a pillow crease in her cheek. To Jonas, she'd never looked more beautiful.

He brushed the back of his hand against her cheek. "Hey."

"Hey back," Kat said, turning to look out at the sea. "It's such a beautiful morning."

"It's not as beautiful as you," Jonas said and he saw surprise flash across her face. She didn't believe him. She didn't even trust what he said. How could he expect her to trust that he'd do as he'd promised once he backed out of the deal? She wouldn't.

A long, taut silence stretched between them and Jonas didn't know how to break it.

Kat did it for him. "What are we doing, Jonas?"

"What do you mean?"

"This. Us. You yanked me out of the theater and we've made love all night after three weeks of avoiding being alone with me. We've always been attracted to each other but..." Her words trailed away.

"But?" he asked.

"But now that we're back in Santa Barbara, this was supposed to be business. Adding sex to the mix just complicates the situation."

"We made love, Kat, you know it and I know it," Jonas said, throwing the statement out there to see how she would react.

She tensed, panic hitting her eyes. "Are you insane? Why are you saying that? We agreed that we wouldn't get personal!"

Her reaction was one of horror and fear. Friggin' *perfect.*

"What is it with you men?" Kat cried, her face flushed with anger. "Why can't you just keep your word, keep it simple? This is why we weren't supposed to get physical, Halstead! It complicates everything. You are not in love with me. I am not in love with you. We're just experiencing an emotional hangover from too much amazing sex."

I am not in love with you.

Right. He got it. At least he had one question answered. He was, apparently, the only one who'd developed feelings, the only one who wanted more than what they'd agreed to.

Crap. Hell. Dammit.

Kat tipped her face up to look at him and it felt like her eyes were drilling down into his soul. What would she see? Would she be able to read him? Kat's eyes widened and she gasped, horrified. "You're having second thoughts. You don't want to get married."

It was his crappy luck that she'd pick up on his reluctance to marry but not on his deepening feelings. Jonas, normally verbally quick, couldn't find the words to explain that he wanted something different, that he still intended to honor their agreement. Kat didn't give him a chance to say anything. Her eyes turned stormy as fury tightened her muscles. Her right hand clenched into a small fist and Jonas wondered if that fist would connect with his body.

"You bastard!" Kat shouted, her hands slapping against his bare chest. "I trusted you! I trusted you to do this. I trusted you to keep your word. I trusted you! Do you not know how hard that was for me? I never thought I'd trust anyone again but I trusted you!"

"Kat, you don't understand…"

Big tears she didn't acknowledge ran down her cheeks. "I can't believe you are bailing on me!"

"Kit-Kat, calm down. We can talk about this, find a solution."

Kat pushed her fist into her sternum and looked

at him, her eyes filled with betrayal. "Oh, God, you really don't want to do this, do you?"

Jonas shook his head. "No, not like this—" He wanted her. He wanted it all.

But she only heard the word *no* because she spun around and flew back into the bedroom.

Jonas followed more slowly, hoping she'd let him explain. Jonas winced when Kat ripped his shirt apart, buttons flying. She pulled her gold dress from the chair, slid it over her head, grabbed her clutch and her shoes and stormed out of the room.

"Will you please calm down?" Jonas asked, and she nailed him with a scorching look. Wrong thing to say. She looked like she was planning his murder.

"Stop talking to me," Kat told him, heading for the front door.

"We can talk about this, find a way forward."

Kat stopped at the door leading to the hallway, her hand on the knob. "The only thing I want from you is for you to show up at the Polo Club on Saturday, in your tux. We'll get married, as we agreed, you'll pay me, as you agreed, and we'll spend the next few months ignoring each other. Got it?"

"Kat—" Jonas shoved his hands into his hair. He wished he could make her listen. But, he realized, Kat was in a full-on temper and nothing he could say, or do, would get through to her.

"We'll talk when you calm down," Jonas said as she yanked the door open and stepped into the hall. "Do you have money for a cab? I can call my driver."

Kat's eyes held the power of a million hurricanes.

"Be there on Saturday. Marry me. Pay me. Surprise me by doing what you said you would. That's all I want. That's all I'll ever want from you."

Ouch.

I am not in love with you...

Jonas watched her walk away from him, barefoot, and felt like there was a knife lodged in his back.

"I'm not doing it."

Jack looked at Jonas, his white eyebrows pulled together. "You're not doing what?"

"Marrying. Dancing to your tune. Giving in to your blackmail," Jonas told his grandfather.

They were in the study at his grandfather's Santa Monica beach house and for the first time in his life Jonas felt free.

"Excuse me?" Jack asked, his tone as cold as the ice cubes he dropped into his bourbon.

"Don't pretend you didn't hear what I said," Jonas retorted. He placed his hands on the back of one of Jack's wing-backed chairs and gave his grandfather a hard stare. "I'm not marrying. Do what the hell you want with your shares. Give them to my father, sell them. But know this—I will not work for Lane, not under any capacity."

"You'll lose the company then," Jack replied, his voice now bland.

"I don't give a crap," Jonas told him. "I'll go out on my own. I'll do something else, *anything* else, but I won't work for that thief again."

Jack looked at him over the rim of his glass, not even slightly surprised by Jonas's hot announcement.

Jonas lifted a finger and pointed it at his grandfather. "You knew he stole funds from the company!"

"It's my company, of course I damn well knew!" Jack replied, annoyed. "The point is when were you going to tell me? And why the hell did you cover it up? Why did you let him skate?"

He knew that, too? Jonas shook his head. He'd thought he'd been so clever keeping it from Jack, yet the wily old man had known it all. Games, Jonas thought, manipulations. He was so tired of it all.

"Probably for the same reason you ignored it. It was easier to let him walk away than to charge him. It was less of a scandal to say that he resigned." Jonas rubbed the back of his neck.

"Why didn't you tell me, Joe?" Jack asked and Jonas frowned at the sadness he heard in his grandfather's voice.

Jack sat in his chair behind his desk, shaking his head. "I thought we were a team, that you trusted me. Obviously you didn't, probably still don't." It was time to tell the truth, Jonas realized, to wipe the slate clean. "I wanted to protect you. I wanted to protect him."

Jack shook his head. "That was my job, to protect you," he protested.

"He's your child."

Jack's expression turned fierce. "You've been more mine than he was. You were always my first priority, my first concern," Jack stated, his voice a soft growl.

"Then why the hell did you insist I marry? Why did you put terms on the shares, on my future?" Jonas demanded, his voice cracking with emotion. "Why would you do that? Haven't I done enough, shown enough loyalty, been good enough?"

"Absolutely," Jonas agreed. "I did it to force you to stand up to me, to choose yourself and what made sense to you. If you had told me to go screw myself nearly three months ago, I could've told you that I'd never pass my shares on to anyone but you, that I was proud of you for finally standing up for yourself."

"I stand up to you all the time! I disagree with you constantly!" Jonas said, his voice rising.

"About business, sure. About your personal life? Not so much. Jonas, you were prepared to marry a stranger because you thought that was what I wanted! It should be, always, about what you want! I wanted you to realize that."

Jonas shook his head, pushing his hand through his hair. "Could you not have just told me that?"

Jack had the temerity to grin. "Not half as much fun. So, are you still going to marry your girl?"

He wished. "No. I love her but she doesn't love me," he reluctantly admitted.

"How do you know?" Jack asked, sounding genuinely interested.

This was the first non-business conversation they'd had in years, Jonas realized.

I am not in love with you...

"She told me that she didn't."

"So make her."

If only it were that simple. "This isn't the caveman era, Jack. Women do make up their own minds these days."

"Well, whether you marry you or not, the shares will be yours."

"I'm not sure I want them now," Jonas replied, the words flying out. He felt as shocked as his grandfather looked. He held up his hand. "I'm not saying that out of spite, Jack, I just don't know if Halstead is what I want to do any more, whether it's part of my future. I can't think of much more than sorting out this mess with Kat," he added.

Jack nodded, looking remarkably sanguine.

"You don't look annoyed. Why aren't you annoyed that I might not want the company?" Jonas asked, frowning.

Jack shrugged. "You're my grandson, you'll do the right thing. For yourself and for the company. Either way, I'll live with it."

Jonas scowled at Jack. "If you die and leave my father the shares, I swear to God I will dig you up and beat you back to death. We clear?"

Jack just smiled and lifted his glass. "Have a drink, Jonas, you sure as hell need one."

Eleven

Kat, hiding out in Tess's apartment, placed her heels on the seat of her chair and wrapped her arms around her shins. She glanced down at her cell phone, saw that her tally of missed calls from Jonas was now at twenty—five for every day they'd been apart.

Kat had taken some vacation time from the restaurant and it had been freely given. Her manager assumed she needed time to make wedding preparations. Since Kat was still answering questions from Mariella Marshall about their "exciting day" and because the tabloids and society columns were still talking about their Cinderella story, Kat presumed the wedding was still on.

She couldn't understand why because Jonas had clearly told her he no longer wanted to get married.

Four days later and she still couldn't understand what she'd done to cause his sudden turnaround.

What was it about her that caused the men in her life to flip out on her? Why couldn't they keep their promises, do what they said they would?

Oh, she was pretty sure Jonas would honor the financial promises he'd made to her. He was still paying for Cath's treatment. But in his touch, in the emotion she saw in his eyes, she'd thought they might have a chance, that he could be someone she could trust with her precious, battered heart.

Kat remembered her question to him—*You really don't want to do this, do you?*—and the image of his shaking head, his guilt-filled eyes. The memory of his heartfelt no was another punch to her heart.

God, why hadn't he just chosen one of his celebrity eye-candy girlfriends for this charade? Why her?

And why did she have to fall in love with him? Why was he the only man who'd managed to slip under the barricade she'd so carefully constructed?

Why couldn't he love her? She was bright and reasonably attractive, albeit stupidly stubborn. And even if he didn't want to remain married to her, why was the notion of marrying her now so unpalatable that he couldn't stand to be hitched to her for a mere ten months? Judging by what he had to lose, that was nothing!

What had she done, said, that made the risk of losing his place at Halstead & Sons an attractive option?

The questions kept bombarding her. Why couldn't she find a man to love her, someone who would put her first, always? Wes hadn't, and she'd been easily and quickly replaced in her father's affections by June. To Jonas, she'd been a way to save his company, a six-million-dollar deal to keep shares worth a billion or two.

She'd loved Wes, adored her father, but what she'd felt for them paled in comparison to how she felt about Jonas.

She beyond loved him.

She loved him with all the harnessed power of the sea, the pull of the moon, the solar flares of the sun. He was everything she wanted and all that she needed. Yet Kat had told him she didn't love him to protect herself. If he couldn't keep his promises, she had to let him go.

And if he wasn't going to stick to their deal, she had to speak to him, to cut the ropes that still held them together. She'd sell the exquisite dresses he'd bought for her online and she'd return his ring. She'd ask him for a payment plan so she could pay off the money he'd already outlaid for Cath's treatment. She'd find the rest of the cash she needed—somewhere.

She could do this. She'd be okay. She'd survived Wes's harsh and warped version of love and her father's neglect. She'd survive Jonas, as well.

The wedding was in three days. It was now or never. Kat picked up her phone and started to type. It was a simple message, three words. Can we meet?

His reply was equally brief. Your apartment. Thirty minutes.

Kat nodded and dropped her phone to the floor. By the end of the afternoon, probably within the hour, she would be saying goodbye to another man she loved.

This was, she thought as tears started to fall, starting to become a habit.

Kat flew out of her car and rushed up the concrete path to her front door, tears still streaming down her face. Through the mist she saw Jonas walking down the steps, his face slack with shock, his eyes red-rimmed.

Kat reached him and threw herself against his chest. "Is it true? Can it be? Please tell me it's not true. I heard it on the radio... They said..."

Jonas's arms held her against him, one hand on the back of her head. "Kit-Kat." He breathed her name into her hair, his grief and worry in every syllable. "Yes, it's true. Harrison had a horrific car accident this morning."

Kat grabbed the lapels of his suit jacket. "Don't tell me he's dead, Jonas! He can't be."

"Let's go inside and I'll tell you what I know."

Kat, her heart weighing a million pounds, led Jonas up the stairs to her apartment and opened the door. He followed her inside and, after tossing a folder onto the coffee table, shrugged off his jacket, pulled off his tie and rolled up his sleeves.

Kat sat on the edge of the couch and stared at her shaking hands, her thoughts going to Harrison in the hospital—her charismatic, funny, driven, kind boss now a shell of the man he'd been the day before.

"He refused to allow me to pay anything toward my rent," Kat said, her voice dropping into the silence between them. "He told me I was doing a great job and he wanted to reward me. So he told me I could have my apartment for free, as part of my compensation."

Jonas sat next to her, his elbows on his knees. "He's a good guy."

"He's a great guy," Kat corrected. "Without him, without my job…" Kat turned her head to look at him. "What happened? Tell me."

Jonas pulled in a deep breath and ran his hand over his face. "He was speeding. You know he has a lead foot. Team that with one of the fastest supercars known to man, it's not a good combination."

"But he's such a good driver. I mean, I heard he could've raced professionally, he was that good," Kat protested.

"Yeah, I don't understand, either. He knew the road, knew the car, and while he was speeding, he was, apparently, not going that fast," Jonas replied. "His car spun out, flipped… He was thrown from the car, which happened to be a good thing. They rushed him straight into surgery."

Kat forced herself to ask the question, not sure she wanted to know the answer. "Is he going to live?"

Jonas shrugged. "He came through the surgery and he's in intensive care. The next few days will tell that story. It doesn't look good, Kat."

"How do you know all this?" Kat asked.

"I spoke to Gabe, his nephew," Jonas replied.

"Dammit." Tears slid down her face again. "He can't die, Jonas. He has so much to live for. Mariella, his kids, his businesses, his staff. He has to be okay."

Jonas placed a hand on her back and Kat had to restrain herself from leaning into him, from looking for his comfort, from soaking in his strength. Her boss was lying in a hospital bed, battered, bloody, hooked up to machines and fighting for his life. His family would be mad with worry. Mariella would be beside herself. Harrison had friends, from all parts of the world, thinking about him, sending him good energy.

If she were in the same situation, who would be worried about her? Tess and Cath? A few work colleagues? She didn't have parents, children, a husband or a lover.

She didn't have Jonas.

Oh, God, she wanted to love him, to be with him. She wanted to be his wife in all the ways that word meant. Not for a few months but forever.

She loved him.

But he didn't want her. Not like that. He wanted out. And could she blame him? This was a crazy situation, one that never really had much of a chance of working. It wasn't his fault he didn't love her like she loved him.

You can't force love…

She had to do this. She had to let him go. If she didn't do it now she didn't know if she ever could.

"We need to talk about Saturday."

Jonas sent her a look that she couldn't interpret. He stood and walked to the window, leaning his shoulder into the wall and looking out onto the street.

Kat started to speak but stopped when Jonas held up a weary hand. "One of the many reasons I've been trying to call you was to tell you that we can't get married on Saturday. It can't happen."

Before she could respond, Jonas spoke again.

"I'm not saying that only because we argued, Kat, there are other, practical, reasons why the wedding can't go ahead. Mariella is coordinating the wedding, and now that Harrison is in ICU, she will be out of action. Even if someone else from MSM Event Planning took over the function, society would expect us to postpone the event. I've known Harrison since I was a kid. He and my grandfather are good friends. Many of his friends are ours and nobody would enjoy themselves. Out of respect for him and his family..."

Kat nodded. She dug her fingers into her waist and said the words that would both break her heart and set them both free. "You should use this extra time to talk to your grandfather. Tell him this isn't going to work. This was a crazy idea and—"

"Jack and I came to an agreement. My being married is no longer a prerequisite to inheriting the shares."

Kat stared at the carpet beneath her feet, fighting the wave of sadness that threatened to pull her under. She had to say the words, get them out. "Then there's no reason for us to marry."

"I'll admit that my reasons for setting us on this

crazy path are no longer valid," Jonas said. He sounded like he was picking his words carefully, like he was trying to let her down gently.

Jonas flicked a glance her way and in the depths of those green eyes she saw an emotion she couldn't identify. It took all of Kat's strength to put a tiny smile on her face. "Well, then, that makes this decision simpler."

Jonas lifted a dark eyebrow. "Really? How?"

"You don't need to get married anymore and you'd save a bundle of cash by calling this off."

Jonas rubbed his fingertips over his forehead. "I never said I wouldn't provide the money I promised. Besides, how else would you pay for Cath's treatment, Kat?"

Kat lifted her heels to the seat of her chair, hoping she was hiding her terror from him. She had no idea how she would pay for it, but that was her problem now, not his. Something would come up; it had to.

"If you could give me a payment plan, I'll repay you as much as I can as soon as I can."

"For God's sake!" Jonas slapped his hand against the wooden frame of the window. "When are you going to realize I don't give a crap about the money? In all this time, have you learned nothing about me?"

I know that you are kind and honorable and you have a big heart. I know that the woman who finally gains your love will be immensely lucky.

"I'm just trying to do the right thing, Jonas," Kat told him, her voice quavering. "I'm trying to make this as easy as possible. I'd like us to walk away as friends."

"Friends?" Jonas repeated the word before thrusting his hand into his hair. "You've got to be freakin' kidding me." He looked at his watch and grimaced in frustration. "I hate to cut this little breakup conversation short, but I have to go. I promised Jack I'd go with him to visit the Marshalls at the hospital. They'll need the support of their friends."

He'd said "breakup," so that made it official. They were over.

Do not cry, Kat. Do not!

Jonas placed his hands in the pockets of his pants and nodded to the folder on the table between them. "It's all in there, Kat. I assumed this discussion would go this way so I made some plans."

Of course he had, he was the CEO of an international company. Making plans was what he did. Kat looked at the folder but didn't reach for it. Even though she'd asked him to come here to end this farce of a relationship, she couldn't bear to see the folder's contents, knowing the papers inside would sever her connection with Jonas.

"Knowing your independent, don't-help-me attitude, you'll probably curse me ten ways to Sunday. But I can't walk out of your life unless I know you will be okay. I had to do it this way, Kat, because giving you the freedom to be happy, to start a new life on your terms, is *that* important to me."

You loving me is all that's important to me!

Kat didn't care about the contents of the folder; she

cared about him. About being with him, loving him. Kat opened her mouth to tell him so, but her words stuck in her throat. She was important to him, she reminded herself, but not important enough to marry.

Kat nodded, wishing he'd stay, wishing she was brave enough to lay her heart on the line. But she wasn't and Jonas, full of honor and integrity, needed to leave.

"'Bye, Kit-Kat."

Her eyes filled with tears and Kat couldn't reply. It took all her willpower to let him cross the short space to the door. He stepped into her hallway and Kat felt like he was dragging her heart behind him. How could she just let him go? How could she allow him to walk out of her life?

Because he didn't want to stay and she couldn't ask him to. Jonas desired her but could never love her and she couldn't settle for less. Not again.

She was worth more than that. He was her fantasy but she wasn't his.

Jonas stopped by the front door, sent her one last look and slipped out of her life.

When the door snicked closed behind him, Kat slipped to the floor and cried.

"Harrison is still in a coma. He's been moved from St. Aloysius Hospital to an undisclosed private clinic. His situation is unchanged."

Kat disconnected the call to her manager and pushed her hair behind her ears. It was her day off and she'd begged him for a shift because she needed to keep her mind occupied, but Jose had refused. This was, he told her, supposed to be the first day of her honeymoon and he'd already arranged the schedule.

Her honeymoon. Kat pulled a face. She and Jonas had talked about going back to Nevis, agreeing that was where they both wanted to be. Instead, she was stuck in her small apartment with nothing to do. Cath was back home and doing relatively well on her new regimen. Kat could visit but Cath would interrogate her about Jonas and she'd be forced to admit they were no longer engaged. That they weren't going to get married.

Apparently, Kat and Jonas were the only two people who knew that their wedding was not simply postponed, as his press release stated, but canceled. Why hadn't he told the world they were over? Conversely, why hadn't she?

Because she didn't really want it to be over and when the news of their breakup hit the public domain, that would truly be the end.

Kat sat on her couch and eyed Jonas's folder, the one he'd left when he'd walked out of her life seventy-two hours before. She hadn't opened it, knowing it would be another confirmation of Jonas's unwillingness to marry her, to create a life with her.

No matter what his press release said, their relationship was over. It was time to accept it, to deal with it, Kat told herself. To do that, she had to face the contents of the folder. So Kat forced herself to pick it up. She placed it on her knees and felt the tears well.

You need to do this. You have to do this. You can't live in this state of limbo forever.

Kat bit her lip and flipped the folder open. The papers were all perfectly aligned and Kat skimmed through them. There was an agreement between Jonas and Whispering Oaks. He'd deposited six million dollars into their account and any monies not used for Cath's treatment were to be donated to cancer research in both her mom's and Cath's names.

Kat placed her hand over her mouth, trying to subdue her sobs. Oh, Jonas. She flipped to another page and saw he had covered the costs for her to go back to school full-time to finish her MBA. He'd prepaid the rent and utilities on her apartment so she could stay there for another year without having to work at the restaurant and he'd bought her a car, a sensible, compact, secondhand SUV with low mileage that was waiting to be collected at a reputable car dealer.

So generous but not over the top. So Jonas. He'd kept his word, down to the letter, as per the original prenup, and he had done it in a way—cleverly, she admitted—she couldn't refuse.

Jonas. She now had everything to make her life easier, but what she most needed was as far away as the moon. She missed him; her cells, her organs, her mind ached for him. She had so much love to give him and nowhere to put it.

Kat sighed, her fingers tapping the pile of papers. Feeling a ridge under what should be flat papers,

Kat lifted the last page of the bulky car insurance papers to see a tiny velvet bag and an envelope with her name written across it. It had been tucked into the corner pocket of the folder.

Kat eyed the envelope while she pulled open the tiny velvet bag, tipping the contents into her palm. The big, square-cut sapphire flashed at her; a deep navy blue that took her breath away. Kat held the ring between her finger and thumb, instantly recognizing the symbolism.

The sapphire was a lot bigger and a deeper blue than her mom's ring, but the design was exactly the same and had her and her mom's initials engraved into the band.

Kat reached for the envelope and ripped the flap open. She pulled out the card and scanned Jonas's hastily penned words.

Kit-Kat,
It's not your mom's, but maybe it will go a little way toward easing the sting of losing her ring.
Unfortunately, the sting of losing you, of what could've been, is going to stay with me forever.
Jonas

Kat read his words and read them again. He didn't want to lose her? He wanted more? Was that what he meant? Could he, possibly, love her?

What did he mean?

Words…words always got in the way.

But if she believed, as she'd always said she did, that people showed how they felt through their actions, then she didn't need his words. Wes had told her, over and over, that he'd loved her, but his actions had proved his statements false. Her father had loved her, but his actions had proved he'd loved June more.

But Jonas, through what he'd done over and over, had expressed his love for her. It was in the way he'd looked at her and in the way he'd touched her, in his concern for her driving a rust-bucket car, needing to know that she was safe. He'd provided the money for Cath's treatment because Kat's worries were his, her family as important as his own. He'd told her he loved her by going to the effort—even though he was a busy man running a huge company—to track down a close copy of her mother's ring.

He hadn't said the words but his actions whispered his love.

She'd just forgotten how to listen. From now on, she *would* listen. She didn't need a marriage, temporary or otherwise, to hear the truth. A marriage agreement wasn't the promise she'd really wanted him to keep, she saw that now.

Instead he'd kept all the important promises. The ones about listening to her and taking care of her because he cared. And for every day he gave her, if he gave her any, she'd listen, and she'd tell him, with words and actions, how much she loved him in return.

She wasn't going to waste another minute. Kat picked up her cell phone and started to track down her man.

* * *

Jonas had felt emotionally battered before but nothing compared to the hell he was currently experiencing five days after walking out of Kat's life.

It will get better, he told himself.

Someday soon it will hurt a little less, and you won't miss her as much.

Jonas, sitting on his surfboard, looked up to his house on the cliff. Returning to Nevis was like returning to the scene of the crime shortly after losing your lover in a knife fight. It was bloody and painful and messy.

Jonas pushed his wet hair back from his face and eyed an incoming wave. Too small, not enough energy.

Not a bad analogy for his life, he thought. He felt small; he lacked energy. Waking up was hard, going to sleep was worse. Staying away from the booze was the hardest of all. But drinking himself into oblivion was too cliché and even though he was in Nevis, hiding out, he still had internet service and a company to run.

A company that was now fully his. The morning after their heart-to-heart conversation, Jack had filed the papers to transfer the shares to Jonas. He'd soon be the majority shareholder of Halstead & Sons. No more interference, no more monthly breakfast meetings—although Jack had hinted that he'd like those to continue.

But the business and Jonas's improved relationship with his grandfather meant little without Kat in his life. Funny how he'd run from the gold diggers and kept his shield up with every woman he'd met, but the simple act of removing a clothing tag had spun Kat into his world. And, while his heart felt like it had been cleaved in two, he couldn't—wouldn't—regret the time he'd spent with her. The past three months had been the best of his life.

Jonas glanced at his watch. It was time to head back to shore. He stretched out on his board and started to paddle in. He supposed he should think about dinner, that he should eat. But food now tasted like cardboard so he probably wouldn't.

Jonas looked toward the stairs leading to his house and frowned when he saw a figure walking down the steps. His steps. He was still far out but the form was female—dark hair, long legs.

He recognized that body, that brightly colored bikini top. He'd pulled that halter top off her torso once or ten times right here in Nevis. Jonas, his heart starting to pound, pumped his arms and his board shot through the water. He kept his eyes on Kat, whose face was covered by a pair of oversize sunglasses. Those had to go, along with her hot-pink top and ripped denim shorts and anything else she was wearing.

She was here and he was never letting her go again.

When he reached the shallows, Jonas pulled his board under his arm and jogged to the beach, stopping only to rip off his ankle cord and toss the board to the sand. He started to run, needing to know why she was there.

Was she here for him or had something happened to Cath? To Harrison? Jack would have called if Harrison had passed on and Jack's calls, and Kat's, obviously, would have been the only ones Jonas answered. There had been none from either of them. Had Kat come to personally deliver some bad news?

God, no.

Jonas stopped and placed his hands on his thighs, not wanting to face whatever she had to say. He didn't think he could take much more heartbreak.

Kat walked toward him and stopped when she was a few feet away. She pushed her hands into the back pockets of her shorts and rocked on her heels.

"I love you."

Jonas heard her words but didn't understand what she was trying to say. So he focused on the one thing he did understand. "You cut your hair."

Kat ran her hand over her funky new hairstyle and lifted an eyebrow. "I fly for hours to tell you that I love you and the first words out of your mouth are about my hair?"

"My brain is spluttering," Jonas admitted. He ran his hand through his hair and sent her an uncertain look. "Are you sure?"

"That I love you? Well, I used the credit card you left me to pay for the ticket," Kat said, pulling her lip between her teeth. "It was hard, but I did it."

Jonas straightened, his hands on his waist, dissecting her words. He'd forgotten that he'd left a credit card with her for emergencies. She hadn't used it once and he'd never expected her to, not with her insistence on independence.

She'd used his card to come to him, to tell him that she loved him. He was that important to her…

Holy crap.

That small gesture told him everything he needed to know. Light, happiness, goddamn relief, slid into him, loosening his knees and causing his throat to constrict. Before he lost his composure, he stepped up to her and ripped the sunglasses off her face. "These are hideous. Say it again."

Kat tipped her head back to meet his gaze, her eyes reflecting wariness and fear. She expected him to reject her and Jonas felt his heart wobble. But he needed to hear her say it again while he looked into her eyes, just to make sure he wasn't losing his mind.

"I love you. I'll keep telling you until you believe me."

Jonas held her precious face in his hands, his thumbs on her cheekbones. "I love you, too."

Kat's hands settled on his waist as she closed her eyes. "Thank God, I thought you might, but I wasn't sure."

Jonas pulled her into his body, her chest pushing into his, her stomach against his fast-growing erection. "How could you not be sure?"

"You didn't tell me," Kat pointed out, love turning her eyes luminous. Jonas started to apologize but Kat placed her fingers on his lips. "But I looked at what you did for me and it was all there. Thank you… Thank you for everything. Cath's treatment. The car. For paying for my studies. The ring. God, the ring."

Jonas looked down at her hands and frowned when he saw the fire opal on her ring finger and the sapphire on her other hand. "You're still wearing my engagement ring."

Kat looked down, lifted her eyebrows and nodded. "It appears I am."

"Why?"

"Why am I wearing the ring?" Kat asked, smiling a little at his question. "Well, I like it and I like being engaged to you. And I figure that until you officially call off our engagement—until our breakup is splashed across tabloids and society columns—then I intend to keep wearing it."

Jonas felt the tension slide from his body. Kat was here. She loved him and his world was perfect.

He smiled. "Well, FYI, hell will ice over before I call off our engagement." He dropped a hot, brief openmouthed kiss on her lips, knowing that if he started to kiss her he wouldn't be able to stop. But he had something he had to do first. They needed to start again…

Kat's joy flashed over her face and pulled her mouth into a wide smile. Then her smile turned to confusion when he took her hands in his and tugged the rings off her fingers.

"What are you doing?" Kat asked him, perplexed.

Jonas didn't answer. He just dropped to one knee,

water still streaming from his body, sand clinging to his calves and thighs.

"No qualifiers, provisos or deals," Jonas said, squinting up at her. "This isn't about my company or my grandfather or a temporary agreement. From that morning on the balcony of my hotel room, I knew I wanted this but I didn't know how to tell you. So… Just you and me, flat-out honest. I love you. I don't want to spend another day without you. Will you marry me?"

"No qualifiers, provisos and deals. Flat-out honest." Kat nodded, her hand on her heart. "Yes."

Jonas's heart sighed as peace and contentment settled over him. He opened his hand and looked at the two rings on his palm. "Choose one for your engagement ring, or if you prefer, we can have something made." He grinned. "Warning, it will probably be expensive."

Kat looked from his face to his palm and back again. She picked up the sapphire ring, slid it back onto the middle finger of her right hand and then picked up the fire opal ring.

"This one. It was the first ring you gave me and the only one I'll ever need. Though a matching wedding band would be nice."

Jonas, his fingers trembling, slid the ring into place and stared down at her hand. When he lifted his head and spoke, he heard the tremble in his voice. He didn't care. "You are my everything, Katrina. The wealth, the success—it means nothing when you're not in my life. You *are* my life."

Kat wound her arms around his neck and kissed the side of his neck. “I’m so happy to be here, with you. Being with you is all I’ll ever need.”

Jonas wrapped his arms tighter around her, happy to stand in the setting sun, the cool breeze on his back and Kat dropping kisses on his neck.

This was peace. Ecstasy. Acceptance. This was who he was supposed to be—the person who loved Kat.

The CEO, the heir, the successful property developer…he was all those things, of course, but being Kat’s lover, friend and husband would forever be his most important jobs. And as her lover, he’d woefully neglected his duties lately.

Jonas bent his knees, scooped Kat up and started to run for the stairs. He couldn’t wait another minute to peel that bikini top off her breasts, shove those denim shorts to the sand.

At the steps Jonas stopped, looked around and remembered this beach was private. He didn’t need to wait any longer than he wanted.

He dropped Kat to her feet and slid his hand under her hair to tug at the strings holding her bikini top in place. Kat surprised him when her hands went for the tie holding up his board shorts. She needed him as much as he needed her and he wanted to weep from joy.

Kat’s fingers brushed against him but he grabbed her hand and lifted it to his mouth, his lips settling on her open palm, his eyes connecting with hers.

“I love you, Kat. Every stubborn, independent,

sexy inch of you. I'm going to make you so damn happy."

Kat's eyes, full of emotion, held the sheen of tears. "Nothing is more important to me than you knowing how much I love you." Kat touched his face. "I think our brand-new engagement is off to a pretty good start."

It was, Jonas thought, because their foundation was, finally, rock-solid. Jonas flashed a wicked grin and guided Kat's hand to where he most wanted it to be.

On a private beach with the woman he loved, who loved him in return—and who also happened to be sexy as hell. What was a man to do?

So Jonas did all of it. And more.

* * * * *

Don't miss the next installment of the
SECRETS OF THE A-LIST *series*

SNOWED IN WITH A BILLIONAIRE
by Karen Booth
Available December 2017!

And pick up these other sexy, sassy romances
from Joss Wood!

TRAPPED WITH THE MAVERICK MILLIONAIRE
PREGNANT BY THE MAVERICK MILLIONAIRE
MARRIED TO THE MAVERICK MILLIONAIRE
HIS EX'S WELL-KEPT SECRET

Available now from Harlequin Desire!

***

If you're on Twitter, tell us what you think
of Harlequin Desire! #harlequindesire

If you enjoyed this book, you'll love
CAN'T HARDLY BREATHE,
the next book in New York Times *bestselling*
author Gena Showalter's
ORIGINAL HEARTBREAKERS *series.*
Read on for a sneak peek!

DANIEL PORTER SAT at the edge of the bed. Again and again he dismantled and rebuilt his Glock 17. Before he removed the magazine, he racked the slide to ensure no ammunition remained in the chamber. He lifted the upper portion of the semiautomatic, detached the recoil spring as well as the barrel. Then he put everything back together.

Rinse and repeat.

Some things you had to do over and over, until every cell in your body learned to perform the task on autopilot. That way, when bullets started flying, you'd react the right way—immediately—without having to check a training manual.

When his eyelids grew heavy, he placed the gun on the nightstand and stretched out across the mattress, only to toss and turn. Staying at the Strawberry Inn without a woman wasn't one of his brightest ideas. Sex kept him distracted from the many horrors that lived inside his mind. After multiple overseas military tours, constant gunfights, car bombs, finding one friend after another blown to pieces, watching his targets collapse because he'd gotten a green light and pulled the trigger…his sanity had long since packed up and moved out.

Daniel scrubbed a clammy hand over his face. In the quiet of the room, he began to notice the mental chorus in the back of his mind. Muffled screams he'd heard since his first tour of duty. He pulled at hanks of his hair, but the screams only escalated.

This. This was the reason he refused to commit to a woman. Well, one of many reasons. He was too messed up, his past too violent, his present too uncertain.

A man who looked at a TV remote as if it were a bomb about to detonate had no business inviting an innocent civilian into his crazy.

He'd even forgotten how to laugh.

No, not true. Since his return to Strawberry Valley, two people had defied the odds and amused him. His best friend slash spirit animal Jessie Kay West… and Dottie.

My name is Dorothea.

She'd been two grades behind him, had always kept to herself, had never caused any trouble and had never attended any parties. A "goody-goody," many had called her. Daniel remembered feeling sorry for her, a sweetheart targeted by the town bully.

Today, his reaction to her endearing shyness and unintentional insults had shocked him. Somehow she'd turned him on so fiercely, he'd felt as if *years* had passed since he'd last had sex rather than a few hours. But then, everything about his most recent encounter with Dot—Dorothea—had shocked him.

Upon returning from his morning run, he'd stood in the doorway of his room, watching her work. As she'd vacuumed, she'd wiggled her hips, dancing to music with a different beat than the song playing on his iPod.

Control had been beyond him—he'd hardened instantly.

He'd noticed her appeal on several other occasions, of course. How could he not? Her eyes, once too big for her face, were now a perfect fit and the most amazing shade of green. Like shamrocks or lucky charms, framed by the thickest, blackest lashes he'd ever seen. Those eyes were an absolute showstopper. Her lips were plump and heart-shaped, a fantasy made flesh. And her body…

Daniel grinned up at the ceiling. He suspected she had serious curves underneath her scrubs. The way the material had tightened over her chest when she'd moved…the lushness of her ass when she'd bent over… Every time he'd looked at her, he'd sworn he'd developed early-onset arrhythmia.

With her eyes, lips and corkscrew curls, she reminded him of a living doll. *Blow her up, and she'll blow me.* He really wanted to play with her.

But he wouldn't. Ever. She lived right here in town.

When Daniel first struck up a friendship with Jessie Kay, his father expressed hope for a Christmas wedding and grandkids soon after. The moment Daniel had broken the news—no wedding, no kids—Virgil teared up.

Lesson learned. When it came to Strawberry Valley girls, Virgil would always think long-term, and he would always be disappointed when the relationship ended. Stress wasn't good for his ticker. Daniel loved the old grump with every fiber of his being, wanted him around as long as possible.

Came back to care for him. Not going to make things worse.

Bang, bang, bang!

Daniel palmed his semiautomatic and plunged to the floor to use the bed as a shield. As a bead of sweat rolled into his eye, his finger twitched on the trigger. The screams in his head were drowned out by the sound of his thundering heartbeat.

Bang, bang!

He muttered a curse. The door. Someone was knocking on the door.

Disgusted with himself, he glanced at the clock on the nightstand—1:08 a.m.

As he stood, his dog tags clinked against his mother's locket, the one he'd worn since her death. He pulled on the wrinkled, ripped jeans he'd tossed earlier and anchored his gun against his lower back.

Forgoing the peephole, he looked through the crack in the window curtains. His gaze landed on a dark, wild mass of corkscrew curls, and his frown deepened. Only one woman in town had hair like that, every strand made for tangling in a man's fists.

Concern overshadowed a fresh surge of desire as he threw open the door. Hinges squeaked, and Dorothea paled. But a fragrant cloud of lavender enveloped him, and his head fogged; desire suddenly overshadowed concern.

Down, boy.

She met his gaze for a split second, then ducked her head and wrung her hands. Before, freckles had covered her face. Now a thick layer of makeup hid them. Unfortunate. He liked those freckles, often imagined—

Nothing.

"Is something wrong?" On alert, he scanned left... right... The hallway was empty, no signs of danger.

As many times as he'd stayed at the inn, Dorothea had only ever spoken to him while cleaning his room. Which had always prompted his early-morning departures. There'd been no reason to grapple with temptation.

"I'm fine," she said, and gulped. Her shallow inhalations came a little too quickly, and her cheeks grew chalk white. "Super fine."

How was her tone shrill and breathy at the same time?

He relaxed his battle stance, though his confusion remained. "Why are you here?"

"I...uh... Do you need more towels?"

"Towels?" His gaze roamed over the rest of her, as if drawn by an invisible force—disappointment struck. She wore a bulky, ankle-length raincoat, hiding the body underneath. Had a storm rolled in? He listened but heard no claps of thunder. "No, thank you. I'm good."

"Okay." She licked her porn-star lips and toyed

with the tie around her waist. "Yes, I'll have coffee with you."

Coffee? "Now?"

A defiant nod, those corkscrew curls bouncing.

He barked out a laugh, surprised, amazed and delighted by her all over again. "What's really going on, Dorothea?"

Her eyes widened. "My name. You remembered this time." When he stared at her, expectant, she cleared her throat. "Right. The reason I'm here. I just… I wanted to talk to you." The color returned to her cheeks, a sexy blush spilling over her skin. "May I come in? Please. Before someone sees me."

Mistake. That blush gave a man ideas.

Besides, what could Miss Mathis have to say to him? He ran through a mental checklist of possible problems. His bill—nope, already paid in full. His father's health—nope, Daniel would have been called directly.

If he wanted answers, he'd have to deal with Dorothea…alone…with a bed nearby…

Swallowing a curse, he stepped aside.

She rushed past him as if her feet were on fire, the scent of lavender strengthening. His mouth watered.

I could eat her up.

But he wouldn't. Wouldn't even take a nibble.

"Shut the door. Please," she said, a tremor in her voice.

He hesitated but ultimately obeyed. "Would you like a beer while the coffee brews?"

"Yes, please." She spotted the six-pack he'd brought with him, claimed one of the bottles and popped the cap.

He watched with fascination as she drained the contents.

She wiped her mouth with the back of her wrist and belched softly into her fist. "Thanks. I needed that."

He tried not to smile as he grabbed the pot. "Let's get you that coffee."

"No worries. I'm not thirsty." She placed the empty bottle on the dresser. Her gaze darted around the room, a little wild, a lot nervous. She began to pace in front of him. She wasn't wearing shoes, revealing toenails painted yellow and orange, like her fingernails.

More curious by the second, he eased onto the edge of the bed. "Tell me what's going on."

"All right." Her tongue slipped over her lips, moistening both the upper and lower, and the fly of his jeans tightened. In an effort to keep his hands to himself, he fisted the comforter. "I can't really tell you. I have to show you."

"Show me, then." *And leave.* She had to leave. Soon.

"Yes," she croaked. Her trembling worsened as she untied the raincoat…

The material fell to the floor.

Daniel's heart stopped beating. His brain short-circuited. Dorothea Mathis was gloriously, wonderfully naked; she had more curves than he'd suspected, generous curves, *gorgeous* curves.

Was he drooling? He might be drooling.

She wasn't a living doll, he decided, but a 1950s

pinup. *Lord save me.* She had the kind of body other women abhorred but men adored. *He* adored. A vine with thorns and holly was etched around the outside of one breast, ending in a pink bloom just over her heart.

Sweet Dorothea Mathis had a tattoo. He wanted to touch. He *needed* to touch.

A moment of rational thought intruded. Strawberry Valley girls were off-limits… His dad…disappointment…but…

Dorothea's soft, lush curves *deserved* to be touched. Though makeup still hid the freckles on her face, the sweet little dots covered the rest of her alabaster skin. A treasure map for his tongue.

I'll start up top and work my way down. Slowly.

She had a handful of scars on her abdomen and thighs, beautiful badges of strength and survival. More paths for his tongue to follow.

As he studied her, drinking her in, one of her arms draped over her breasts, shielding them from his view. With her free hand, she covered the apex of her thighs, and no shit, he almost whimpered. Such bounty should *never* be covered.

"I want…to sleep with you," she stammered. "One time. Only one time. Afterward, I don't want to speak with you about it. Or about anything. We'll avoid each other for the rest of our lives."

One night of no-strings sex? Yes, please. He wanted her. Here. Now.

For hours and hours…

No. No, no, no. If he slept with the only maid at

the only inn in town, he'd have to stay in the city with all future dates, over an hour away from his dad. What if Virgil had another heart attack?

Daniel leaped off the bed to swipe up the raincoat. A darker blush stained Dorothea's cheeks…and spread…and though he wanted to watch the color deepen, he fit the material around her shoulders.

"You…you don't want me." Horror contorted her features as she spun and raced to the door.

His reflexes were well honed; they had to be. They were the only reason he hadn't come home from his tours of duty in a box. Before she could exit, he raced behind her and flattened his hands on the door frame to cage her in.

"Don't run," he croaked. "I like the chase."

Tremors rubbed her against him. "So…you want me?"

Do. Not. Answer. "I'm in a state of shock." And awe.

He battled an insane urge to trace his nose along her nape…to inhale the lavender scent of her skin…to taste every inch of her. The heat she projected stroked him, sensitizing already desperate nerve endings.

The mask of humanity he'd managed to don before reentering society began to chip.

Off-kilter, he backed away from her. She remained in place, clutching the lapels of her coat.

"Look at me," Daniel commanded softly.

After an eternity-long hesitation, she turned. Her gaze remained on his feet. Which was probably a good thing. Those shamrock eyes might have been his undoing.

"Why me, Dorothea?" She'd shown no interest in him before. "Why now?"

She chewed on her bottom lip and said, "Right now I don't really know. You talk too much."

Most people complained he didn't talk enough. But then, Dorothea wasn't here to get to know him. And he wasn't upset about that—really. He hadn't wanted to get to know any of his recent dates.

"You didn't answer my questions," he said.

"So?" The coat gaped just enough to reveal a swell of delectable cleavage as she shifted from one foot to the other. "Are we going to do this or not?"

Yes!

No! Momentary pleasure, lifelong complications. "I—"

"Oh, my gosh. You actually hesitated," she squeaked. "There's a naked girl right in front of you, and you have to think about sleeping with her."

"You aren't my usual type." A Strawberry Valley girl equaled marriage. No ifs, ands or buts about it. The only other option was hurting his dad, so it wasn't an option at all.

She flinched, clearly misunderstanding him.

"I prefer city girls, the ones I have to chase," he added. Which only made her flinch again.

Okay, she hadn't short-circuited his brain; she'd liquefied it. Those curves…

Tears welled in her eyes, clinging to her wealth of black lashes—gutting him. When Harlow Glass had tortured Dorothea in the school hallways, her cheeks had burned bright red but her eyes had remained dry.

I hurt her worse than a bully.

"Dorothea," he said, stepping toward her.

"No!" She held out her arm to ward him off. "I'm not stick thin or sophisticated. I'm too easy, and you're not into pity screwing. Trust me, I get it." She spun once more, tore open the door and rushed into the hall.

This time, he let her go. His senses devolved into hunt mode, as he'd expected, the compulsion to go after her nearly overwhelming him. *Resist!*

What if, when he caught her—and he *would*—he didn't carry her back to his room but took what she'd offered, wherever they happened to be?

Biting his tongue until he tasted blood, he kicked the door shut.

Silence greeted him. He waited for the past to resurface, but thoughts of Dorothea drowned out the screams. Her little pink nipples had puckered in the cold, eager for his mouth. A dark thatch of curls had shielded the portal to paradise. Her legs had been toned but soft, long enough to wrap around him and strong enough to hold on to him until the end of the ride.

Excitement lingered, growing more powerful by the second, and curiosity held him in a vise grip. The Dorothea he knew would never show up at a man's door naked, requesting sex.

Maybe he didn't actually know her. Maybe he should learn more about her. The more he learned, the less intrigued he'd be. He could forget this night had ever happened.

He snatched his cell from the nightstand and dialed Jude, LPH's tech expert.

Jude answered after the first ring, proving he hadn't been sleeping, either. "What?"

Good ole Jude. His friend had no tolerance for bull, or pleasantries. "Brusque" had become his only setting. And Daniel understood. Jude had lost the bottom half of his left leg in battle. A major blow, no doubt about it. But the worst was yet to come. During his recovery, his wife and twin daughters were killed by a drunk driver.

The loss of his leg had devastated him. The loss of his family had changed him. He no longer laughed or smiled; he was like Daniel, only much worse.

"Do me a favor and find out everything you can about Dorothea Mathis. She's a Strawberry Valley resident. Works at the Strawberry Inn."

The faint *click-clack* of typing registered, as if the guy had already been seated in front of his wall of computers. "Who's the client, and how soon does he—she?—want the report?"

"I'm the client, and I'd like the report ASAP."

The typing stopped. "So this is personal," Jude said with no inflection of emotion. "That's new."

"Extenuating circumstances," he muttered.

"She do you wrong?"

I'm not stick thin or sophisticated. I'm too easy, and you're not into pity screwing. Trust me, I get it.

"The opposite," he said.

Another pause. "Do you want to know the names of the men she's slept with? Or just a list of any criminal acts she might have committed?"

He snorted. "If she's gotten a parking ticket, I'll be shocked."

"So she's a good girl."

"I don't know what she is," he admitted. Those corkscrew curls…pure innocence. Those heart-shaped lips…pure decadence. Those soft curves… *mine, all mine.*

"Tell Brock this is a hands-off situation," he said before the words had time to process.

What the hell was wrong with him?

Brock was the privileged rich boy who'd grown up ignored by his parents. He was covered in tats and piercings and tended to avoid girls who reminded him of the debutantes he'd been expected to marry. He preferred the wild ones…those willing to proposition a man.

"Warning received," Jude said. "Dorothea Mathis belongs to you."

He ground his teeth in irritation. "You are seriously irritating, you know that?"

"Yes, and that's one of my better qualities."

"Just get me the details." Those lips…those curves… "And make it fast."

CAN'T HARDLY BREATHE—available soon from Gena Showalter and HQN Books!

It's almost Christmas when Dani is snowed in with her too-sexy boss—and an abandoned baby wearing a note that says he's the father! Nathaniel needs Dani's help, but playing house means finally facing the desire they can no longer deny...

Read on for a sneak peek of BILLIONAIRE BOSS, HOLIDAY BABY by USA TODAY *bestselling author Janice Maynard, part of Harlequin Desire's #1 bestselling* ***BILLIONAIRES AND BABIES*** *series.*

This was a hell of a time to feel arousal tighten his body.

Dani looked better than any woman should while negotiating the purchase of infant necessities during the beginnings of a blizzard with her brain-dead boss and an unknown baby.

Her body was curvy and intensely feminine. The clothing she wore to work was always appropriate, but even so, Nathaniel had found himself wondering if Dani was as prim and proper as her office persona would suggest.

Her wide-set blue eyes and high cheekbones reminded him of a princess he remembered from a childhood storybook. The princess's hair was blond. Dani's was more of a streaky caramel. She'd worn it up today in a sexy knot, presumably because of the Christmas party.

HDEXP092017

While he stood in line, mute, Dani fussed over the contents of the cart. “If the baby wakes up,” she said, “I’ll hold her. It will be fine.”

In that moment, Nathaniel realized he relied on her far more than he knew and for a variety of complex reasons he was loath to analyze.

Clearing his throat, he fished out his wallet and handed the cashier his credit card. Then their luck ran out. The baby woke up and her screams threatened to peel paint off the walls.

Dani’s smile faltered, but she unfastened the straps of the carrier and lifted the baby out carefully. “I’m so sorry, sweetheart. Do you have a wet diaper? Let’s take care of that.”

The clerk pointed out a unisex bathroom, complete with changing station. The tiny room was little bigger than a closet. They both pressed inside.

They were so close he could smell the faint, tantalizing scent of her perfume.

Was it weird that being this close to Dani turned him on? Her warmth, her femininity. Hell, even the competent way she handled the baby made him want her.

That was the problem with blurring the lines between business and his personal life.

HDEXP092017